THE BOUNDARY WALKER

Deryk Cameron Stronach

Copyright © 2020 Deryk Stronach

All rights reserved. No part of this book may be reproduced in any form or by any electronic or mechanical means, including information storage and retrieval systems, without written permission from the author, except in the case of a reviewer, who may quote brief passages embodied in critical articles or in a review.

Trademarked names appear throughout this book. Rather than use a trademark symbol with every occurrence of a trademarked name, names are used in an editorial fashion, with no intention of infringement of the respective owner's trademark. The information in this book is distributed on a "as is" basis, without warranty. Although every precaution has been taken in the preparation of this work, neither the author nor the publisher shall have any liability to any person or entity with respect to any loss or damage caused or alleged to be caused directly or indirectly by the information contained in this book.

This work is fiction, Names, characters, places, and incidents either are the product of the author's imagination or are used fictitiously, and any resemblance to any actual persons, living or dead, events, or locales is entirely coincidental.

Acknowledgements

Thanks to Mrs Sreenivasan Jayandi (Mrs Pathy), Mr Sheik Alaudin Mohd Ismail and Jim Walker for their invaluable criticism and comments.

Thanks to Felix Cheong for his tutorship, for correcting my previous work and offering encouragement.

Special thanks to Mary Baey for putting up with my ramblings while I worked my way through the many generations of this story. She gave me the room to breathe and create.

The Boundary Walker

Contents

Prologue 7
A Holiday Romance 9
The Firth of Clyde 15
A Quiet Night 18
A Couple of Travellers 27
An Unwanted Gift 31
The Vet 35
The Brothers Ginger 38
Getting to Know You 44
Visit from an Old Friend 47
Taking the Queen's Shilling 53
Captain Macduff 59
A Most Peculiar Department 65
A Most Unusual List 71
History Repeating Itself 75
Going on a Cruise 83
Mermaids and Submarines 96
Major 100
The Dog Walker 109
A Flight of Fantasy 115

Go West	122
The Master's Master	127
Two Revealed	138
A Gift Revealed	143
A Bit over the Top	147
Unwelcome Dinner Guests	151
Skinny Dipping	160
A Brigadier Came a Visiting	165
Night Nurse	176
A Plan is Needed	180
A Simply Complicated Plan	186
Tidying Up	193
Black and White Movies.	204
Pranksters	212
Should Auld Acquaintance…	225
Straight from the Horse's Mouth	242
The Homecoming	250
A Private Shopping Trip	256
The Job Interview	264
A New Recruit	270
Hide and Secrets	283
Graveyard of the Dead Iron Fishes	293
Planning, Logistics and Intrigue	307
A Traitor Exposed	315
The Prelude to an Operation	325

Boat Away	335
Boat Up, Boat Down	341
Baby Sub	346
The First Arrivals	350
Epilogue	369

PROLOGUE

The story surrounding the spate of kidnappings in Scotland by the mythical aquatic shapeshifting creatures called kelpies did not start with Emma. Still, every story requires a beginning, so this story starts with a romantic dreamer called Emma.

What is important is not the actual kidnapping of Emma, a fact which may or may not be a tragedy, but why?

The protagonist in this story is a retired military intelligence officer, a Lt. Col. Hamish Hamilton. Hamilton, gifted with second sight, was a Boundary Walker, one who could see some that had passed, some that were going to pass and creatures that others thought were only legends. Legends live if you know where and how to look for them.

Hamilton's burden was that he knew.

A Holiday Romance

When she stepped off the ferry onto the concrete ramp on the Isle of Cumbrae, Emma Lafferty flipped a mental coin in her head and decided to walk around the island anti-clockwise. Once she had circumvented the island, she would end up in the same place so, in the end, it would make no real difference.

She had arrived in Largs, Ayrshire the night before and had spent a cosy night in her one-bedroom Airbnb apartment on Nelson Street. Leaving her luggage in the apartment, she had a breakfast of a bacon roll and black coffee in the Green Shutters Bistro down by the waterfront. As she breakfasted, she had watched the ferry plying to and fro across the short gap between the mainland and the small island. She had decided that the weather was ideal for a walk, fresh and sunny and with a fair chance of remaining so for the rest of the day. She paid her bill and walked to the ferry terminal.

Emma had never been on a ferry before. It was fun. Excitement made her feet tingle or was it the engine throbbing in the bowels of the ferry. The water had been calm and the beginning of her adventure too short, she barely had time to walk around the viewing areas. She had taken some selfies and panoramic shots with her phone. It was for this experience she had travelled north to Scotland, its wide-open spaces, beautiful scenery, fresh air and everything that Birmingham was not. Dumping Tommy and going on a holiday by herself was her best idea yet. The two-timing bastard that he was. He was her past. She was young, single and free. She imagined how she looked with her carefully dyed short blond hair, a red tartan scarf bought at Glasgow airport, a beige wind-cheater jacket and skin-tight jeans that she had struggled for ten minutes on the bed to squeeze into, her second skin. She wore short high heeled boots. Maybe not the best footwear for walking and they were not that comfortable, but she liked them, and that is what mattered.

There were no pavements, but the sparse traffic made walking safe. Emma walked on the right, facing any potential oncoming traffic. Of the bikes and cars, the bikes were probably the more dangerous, being ridden by tourists who had last ridden many years before. The roadside flowers were vibrant, and hidden birds chirped and tweeted. A friend had visited Millport, Isle of Cumbrae last year and had raved about it and Emma began to see why. This landscape was not Birmingham, not by a long chalk.

Emma reached the northernmost point of the island and stopped for a short while to take a couple of selfies by the HMS[1] Sheerwater sailor's memorial monument at Tomont End. Walking on, she followed the road as it curved away to the south-west. She passed White Bay and Wine Bay lying next to the road. She did not know their names, but she loved the views. She loved the calming sound of the waves gently splashing on the stony beaches. It was all just so natural.

As she passed Stinking Bay, she heard someone singing. It was beautiful, a young male voice, crisp and clear; captivating. Curious,

---

[1] Her Majesty's Ship

she stopped walking and without thinking went to investigate. She had noticed that on some places the shoreline came right up to the road, in others, the water's edge lay back obscured by bushes. She found a pathway through the mixed gorse bushes and wildflowers and stepped through, following the voice. Her newly found curiosity to find a new life drove her on. It crossed her mind again that maybe her high-heeled boots were not built for following rocky coastal paths, but fashion required sacrifices, she was in control of her life and was free to go where she wanted and to do what she wanted. It was freedom. It was exhilarating.

Coming out of the bushes, she looked for the singer. She guessed he was behind the rocks a short distance off. As she scrambled over the rocks her heel finding every dent and crevice, she played in her mind the possible excuses she would use if she were spotted. She was not so much spotted as touched when she stumbled over the young man. She jumped back with alacrity and growing embarrassment.

The dark-haired tanned young man was about her age. He had stopped singing. They stared at each other for a few moments until he signalled with his hand for her to join him. She did. While she felt she did not have a choice, it just seemed so natural. She sat facing him looking into his deep sparkling emerald green eyes. He started to sing again, and she just sat and listened, transfixed, mesmerised. She thought without thinking too deeply that he had a beautiful voice, like the sound of nature, so natural.

As the song came to an end, he stood up and held out his hand. She stood and went to him, and they embraced and kissed. She never wondered why he was naked. She had no fear. It just felt so natural. As they parted, he took her hand and led her to the water's edge, and they entered the cold River Clyde waters. She did not feel the cold she was in her dream. It was just so natural.

Two days later, two German boys following the shoreline found what they thought initially to be a strange jellyfish. After poking it with a stick a couple of times, they realised that it was something else and they did not like what they thought it was. Neither did the police. Human lungs did not belong on the Clyde shore except in a human.

The Firth of Clyde

There is an inverted heart-shaped small island in the mouth or firth of the River Clyde on the west coast of Scotland called the Isle of Cumbrae. It would take you about two hours to bicycle around or a good four hours at a comfortable walk. It stands off a short ten-minute ferry ride from a town called Largs on the Scottish mainland. Cumbrae has one town, Millport, nestling in the sheltered south of the island.

Both towns were famous in their time as Victorian seaside resorts, especially for tourists from the city of Glasgow and the other industrial towns in the centre of lowland Scotland. In days gone by, tourists would stay at one of the many hotels or boarding houses. The advent of cheap travel abroad took away many of the tourists and most of the hotels were not needed. Millport was particularly hit by the roll on roll off ferry service from Largs as visitors no longer needed to stay on the island, but could travel down by train from

Glasgow in the morning, hop on the ferry to the island, take the waiting bus to Millport and return that evening. As day-trippers increased on sunny days or holiday weekends, the hotels were no longer required, and they gradually died away one by one.

Nowadays, only one or two hotels are remaining. The growing trend is to Airbnb.

Largs and Millport survive on the visitors and have adjusted to survive. They are still quiet in the winter months and bustling in the summer. Some shops have two opening schedules, one for summer and one for winter. As for spring and autumn, it depends on the weather. An unexpected sunny day can bring out the tourists in their shorts, tee-shirts and sunglasses quicker than it takes a slurping ice-cream to melt. Fish and chips from the many 'chippies' supply copious amounts throughout the year, but like most businesses, their profits come from the summer trade and public holidays.

A large number of retirees make Largs and Millport their home, in many cases, their last home. It is a safe place where everybody is friendly, and life has an aura of comfortable normality about it. Nothing dangerous ever happens there. Usually, that is, but things change in a wind's whisper.

Hamish Hamilton, known as Ham as long as he could remember, spent his childhood on the island and his adult life in the military or government service until he too had retired to Largs. Life seemed to turn a full circle. Too many people on the quiet island knew too much or cared too much what other people were doing. After the life, he had led, and the mental trauma he had suffered, he needed the anonymity of a town the size of Largs. He needed the peace, tranquillity and self-imposed solitude it offered. It had the advantage that it was big enough that he could hide in the crowd. Although sociable if approached, he was happy to be left alone. Retirement in Largs suited him nicely.

A Quiet Night

She danced backwards and forwards as if she was trying to run on the water. The sun sparkled on the waves as they lapped at her ankles, and she giggled in the pleasure of the cool water on her warm skin. In and out of the water and onto the white sand she ran, skipped and jumped, sometimes leaping backwards, other times turning and stumbling up the sandy beach. The water always won, catching her, wetting her calves. In and out she danced, twisting and turning, laughing. Her hand that was not holding her short dress away from the water flicked away the short unruly brown hair as it flopped across her face.

She was happy, and this made Ham happy. It was not his habit to smile. He was guarded with his smiles. She had often chided him for his apparent seriousness. In the beginning, she had played and joked around trying to force a smile but had realised quite early in their relationship that with Ham, a calm demeanour was as good as it got. He did not show emotions.

Ham realised that even her laughter sounded French. Somewhere in his mind, he began to consider this. He had never thought about it before. Suzanne was French, but he never thought about her heritage or nationality. It was just what she was, French. She was just the quirky, funny and sometimes overly humorous woman who had captured his heart. She was his very own bundle of joy and sometimes pain in the ass. He loved her deeply and was content to watch her antics.

Slowly, but much too quickly, the scene dissolved in front of his eyes. He tried to claw it back, but it faded and dragged him back into reality. It grew darker and colder. It was night-time on the Scottish west coast, his home since retirement. He was dragged unwillingly back to reality. Ham's face changed slightly with the untimely return to the real world. Those who did not know him may not have noticed, but those that did would know it was a good time to be elsewhere. He straightened up from the railing where he had been leaning, looking down onto the dark pebbly beach of a chilled Largs Bay on a mid-September evening and slowly turned. Ham was not a happy bunny.

Ham's eyes sought and focused on the noisy distraction that had broken the spell. The ruckus had awoken him from his dream. A dream he had enjoyed.

Two youths, early to mid-twenties, white, the younger one blond, the other with a mop of ginger hair, Glaswegians judging by their voices were teasing and tormenting the cat-woman. Ham did not particularly like the cat-woman, but these idiots had picked the wrong time and place to play their obnoxious games. He was upset that these morons had ruined his pleasant evening. It would take a lot of self-control for this to end peaceably.

Cat-woman, as was her wont, had one of her cats on a leash, held this time protectively in her arms against her ample chest.

While the dog walkers would storm up and down the Largs' promenade, she walked her cats. The regular dog owners nodded to her as one would a simpleton with condescending smiles. She didn't seem to notice or care. The short, plump Afro-Caribbean woman with chubby cheeks and an infectious smile was happy in her little world, and her world was cats. She greeted everyone pleasantly and even talked to the odd dog. The dogs just accepted or avoided her.

The two noisy youths took turns in trying to either poke the cat or try to take it away from her. When this failed, they called her names and swore loudly at the cowering woman. Separated, the two boys tried to get at the cat in a flanking movement from both sides at once, which caused the woman to squeak out aloud in her high-pitched voice. Her clamour only seemed to encourage the boys.

Ham had had about enough. He had come out for a quiet evening's stroll. He had wanted solitude and quiet, and he ended up with this nonsense. He walked towards the raucous disturbance. At first, the boys had not seemed to notice him. It was evening, the area near the boating pond devoid of sufficient lighting, and they were too engrossed in their fun and games.

"Enough," he said quietly but firmly. "You've had your fun. Enough. Leave the lady and her pet alone and walk away."

The two youths stopped suddenly. They appeared shocked that there was anyone else there and even more surprised that this person should dare to interfere with their entertainment. They studied him for a few moments, surprised. The ginger was the first to recover. He started to laugh. It was the loud, braying laugh of a bully. The blond looked at the ginger who appeared to be the leader and sought a cue for what to do next.

The ginger grabbed hold of the cat woman's shoulders from behind and shouted, "Get him, John!" John seemed hesitant. He looked at Ham, an old grey-bearded man, in a dark Barbour jacket and grey Kangol flat cap. Ham was slightly shorter than the youth John, and he was older. Much older.

"Go on!" encouraged the ginger-haired youth. "Get him!"

"Stop it now, boy," said Ham to John, quietly, slightly hoarsely. "You'll get hurt. Walk away from the woman and the cat, and that's the end of it. Don't listen to him. He's an idiot. Just walk away." John looked at ginger again, who nodded his head at Ham in a motion that said get on with it.

John stepped forward and started to swing at Ham. Ham could see it coming a mile away. The inexperience was embarrassing. He cupped the palm of his hand and began to slap John on the side of his head. His target was at the lad's ear, but at the last moment, he opened the cupped hand slightly and slapped him firmly on the temple. It was enough to send John falling senseless to the ground. Ham had learned not to punch as they show in the movies as this might damage the trigger finger, but to slap hard and firm with a cupped hand, 'Slappy-Jappy' he called it. Some things you do not forget. Ham had practised long and hard, and this had long ago become an instinct.

Even while John was falling, Ham moved forward to pull the ginger away from the Cat-woman. The carrot-topped youth looked surprised. Cat -tried to get her cat out of the way, and this distraction allowed time for the ginger to step back out of Ham's reach. The ginger reached into his pocket and pulled out a knife. He pushed a switch and a blade folded out and locked into place with a click. Suddenly the ginger was all smiles again. He waved the knife around in front of himself so that Ham could not miss it. The youth wanted to intimidate Ham with the knife, but all Ham saw was an amateur showing lack of skill. Ham's expression did not change. He just waited for the ginger to make the next move, then it would be over. The youth thrust his right arm forward expecting an easy stab, but Ham pushed the knife hand easily out of the way with his left forearm and with his right shoved a straight finger jab up deep into the ginger's solar plexus. The knife fell as the youth let out a gasp of air. The ginger's head came down, and Ham brought his knee up and contacted the poor boy's nose. Ham could hear and feel it break on his knee with a clack and a squishing sound. Ham raised his right hand to chop at the nape of the ginger's neck but stopped.

Ham left it at that. They were only a couple of punk kids. Twenty-something years old, with minds of adolescent youths. He didn't want to hurt them any more than he had to. He picked up the knife and closing it, threw it far out into the water.

He told the Cat-woman to go and not mention what had happened. He said it would not happen again and that nothing serious had happened. The boys would be fine. She nodded and scuttled off, but Ham found the look on her face as she did so slightly puzzling. It was not the face of a frightened woman; it held the expression of someone who had seen what she had expected. The expression seemed to display a confirmation. It was only fleeting, and Hamilton let it slip, it seemed unimportant at that time. Ham turned and checked on the two boys. The ginger-haired youth was rolling on the floor whimpering. John, the blond, was sat up, shaking his head, trying to clear the cobwebs.

On a whim, Ham bent down and said, "Don't mess with a vet kid." And with that, he walked away towards Largs town. Part of him felt like a bully, but they had attacked him first, and they had tried to use a knife. End of story as far as he was concerned.

A Couple of Travellers

Another couple narrowly escaped being enmeshed in the story of the kelpie kidnappings. Freddie and Jacky became close friends from the day they started their studies at Glasgow University. Freddie's family had money to throw at their son, and Freddie carried on the family tradition, throwing it onward to anything that took his fancy. A bright red Ferrari ate the money in insurance, petrol and service charges, but Freddie regarded it as a necessity. He loved the car as it gave him freedom and status. Jacky loved the car as it gave them time together.

Taking a break from their studies, they had driven across Scotland to Edinburgh, up to Inverness, staying at the Royal Highland Hotel with its famous large open staircase, westwards following Loch Ness, without sighting the monster, and down to Loch Lomond to the splendour of the stately Cameron House. After a couple of days of fine dining and luxury surroundings, they drove south to Glasgow, but not wanting their mini holiday to end so soon, they decided to day-trip to Cumbrae and Millport.

Freddie was a little bit worried that the angle of the slipway at Largs onto the Cumbrae ferry might damage the bottom of the sportscar. He was not worried about the cost, but the time his beloved car might be under repair made him queasy. Jacky talked him into taking the gamble. He need not have worried as the car drove on and off without incident.

Driving around the island, they parked in Millport and wandered around. After having a coffee and a bite to eat in the Garrison House café, they visited the museum which was next door. In the museum, an exhibit explained that the island once hosted one end of the anti-submarine net and 'Hush-hush' during World War Two. On a whim, Jacky wanted to hunt down these historical sights, and as they were on the route back to the ferry, Freddie agreed.

Half an hour later they stood beside the parked Ferrari looking over the bushes towards Skate Point. At Jacky's insistence, they weaved their way through the gorse bushes to the rocky shore. It was Jacky that found the young dark-skinned girl sunbathing nude on a flat rock, hidden from the road. She was singing softly almost to herself. He excused himself profusely even as Freddie bumped into him. The girl just smiled.

Apologising again, Jacky and Freddie made to move off. The girl stood up and held up her hands in an inviting gesture to them both. Her singing increased in volume. Jacky and Freddie looked at each other and smiled conspiratorially.

"Sorry, dear, but we are not that way inclined." And with a giggle, Jacky hurried Freddie off to their car, the ferry and their bachelor love-nest in Glasgow.

It was more a close shave than either of the young men could imagine. Over thirty-seven thousand people go missing in Scotland each year, with seven hundred and thirty classified as long term missing. A few more or less might be lost in the figures. No-one knew what had happened, or what might have happened because nothing happened this time, but next time might be a different story.

There was a problem on the Clyde.

An Unwanted Gift

Late that evening, Ham turned left out of his tenement building and walked along the Ayrshire Coastal Path by Castle Bay to the Largs Pencil Monument about two and a half kilometres away. The monument commemorates the battle between the Vikings and the Scots in 1263.

Every September Largs celebrates this battle and the town suddenly bursts at the seams with tourists wanting to see the Viking Village, the Viking march along the promenade with flaming torches and the burning of the Viking longship with the said torches. Or they just wanted to enjoy the fairground on the town's seaside car park by the promenade, which was a bit of crazy planning, as the extra visitors then had nowhere left to park their cars. Somehow, they managed. That was why, during this period, Ham chose to walk late in the late evenings when it was quieter. He did not come to live in Largs for the crowds of humanity. He came for a peaceful retirement. Maybe, he thought, he should go somewhere else for future Septembers. Ham saw that a few people, possibly with the same frame of mind, out walking their dogs in the evenings.

As he passed the Pencil, he encountered a short dark figure. He knew the shape and dreaded the conversation.

"Mr Ham," she started, "I have been looking for you." she sang in her Caribbean lilt. Ham groaned silently in his head. He had not realised that he was so famous. How did she know him? He did not say anything. To talk to her was to encourage her and once again, he was not in the mood to talk to anyone, especially the Cat-woman. How would he address her anyway? He only knew her as Cat-woman. He waited.

"I have been thinking about you. I have seen you often here. Always walking alone. You are a very sad and lonely man." Ham stared at her. It was worse than he had imagined.

"I am grateful for what you did for Tiddles and me." Nobody called their cat Tiddles did they? She continued. "You were a bit rough with those boys, but they were naughty, so I guess what you did was alright. Anyway, I have something for you." She started to dig into her voluminous bag, leading Ham to begin to protest. He did not want her money. He put his hands up to signal her to stop. The voiced objection died in his throat. He stood in horror. She had taken out a kitten and put it in his hands: a grey and black striped furball with bright blue eyes that seemed too big for its face.

"Meow," went the cat.

"What the f...." Ham looked up and received two small tins of cat food from the cat-woman. "What?" He paused as he slowly recovered. "Lady, I..." But she had disappeared into the dark.

"It's alright. No need to thank me." Came a voice from the darkness.

Ham looked at the kitten.

"Meow." It said. It purred, closed its blue eyes and promptly fell asleep.

"Oh shit." Ham looked up at the heavens for a few minutes. He would give it back to her tomorrow. He put the small kitten into the left pocket of his olive-green Barbour jacket, the two cans in the right and walked on. Thank goodness for the Barbour's large pockets. Why didn't he tell her to take the damned cat?

The Vet

The next night, Ham decided to turn right out of his door and head along the promenade past the silent fairground and empty Viking village towards the point at the boating pond.

He had just walked past the RNLI[2] Slipway when a figure approached him. Ham only wanted a peaceful life. He thought he might see the Cat-woman and be able to hand the kitten back. What did surprise him was, he thought it would be the ginger-haired youth from a couple of nights ago that would approach for a rematch, not the blond John. Ham prepared himself. The youth stopped a couple of meters in front and looked down at the ground as if gathering his thoughts. He looked up.

"What we did was wrong. We should have left the Cat-woman alone." Ham realised that other people probably called her the Cat-

---

[2] Royal National Lifeboat Institute

woman as well. He continued, "We should have walked away when you said. Sorry about the cat. I wouldn't have hurt it. Honest. And you being a vet and all. No wonder you were upset." It took a few seconds for the pieces to click into place.

"I'm a veteran, not a veterinarian." The boy looked blank. "I'm ex-military, not a bloody animal doctor."

"Oh."

"Meow." Came the muffled voice.

"What?"

"Nothing."

"Anyway, I wanted to tell you, Gregor, that's the guy I was with a couple of nights ago. He's up the path with his two brothers. They're waiting for you. Gregor and his family are not from here. They're from the city. They're big in the gangs." He paused for a while. "Just thought I'd tell you so you could walk away. Thought I'd give you a chance."

"Thanks, kid. I appreciate it. Tell me, do you like cats?"

"I'm allergic. Cats break me out. Why?"

"Meow."

"What?"

"Nothing. Thanks, kid. On you go." The boy looked at him as if he was expecting him to turn and walk back. "It's ok; I can deal with it." The boy nodded and walked away.

"Meow."

"Shush." Ham thought this might happen. He had thought the ginger to be the vindictive type. As he walked on, he ran through a few plans in his head. He considered walking away, but he would never know when they might decide to "pay him a visit" again. Best to get it over with tonight when he was ready.

The Brothers Ginger

There were only three of them, Gregor the ginger with a plaster holding some padding on his swollen red nose beneath a couple of lovely black eyes, fat ginger and skinny ginger. The brothers were older and had the hard look of the city streets about them. That they came from Glasgow was obvious as soon as they opened their mouths.

"Hey, you. I want to talk to you."

"Yes?"

"Meow."

"What?'

"You said you wanted to talk to me. Go ahead. I'm listening."

"You beat up my little kid brother. I'm going to do you for that."

"Well, he did try to stick me with a knife. I thought that was a bit naughty."

"You tried to stick him, did you?" fat ginger said to Gregor the ginger. He said it with an expression of pride which sickened Ham. "Where's your knife?" Ham realised that Gregor the ginger was expected to produce it and use it this evening.

"He took… I dropped it. John said this guy threw it in the water." The expression of pride disappeared. Fat ginger dug into his pocket and handed Gregor a flat folded razor, which the ginger-haired took and opened. A gleeful smile grew over the exposed face.

Fat ginger and skinny ginger also took out razors. It was the one that skinny ginger took out that caught Ham's eye; he had two flat razors bound together. That was just evil. In a razor fight, most injuries were on the face, arms and abdomen. A slicing cut by a razor is painful, but it leaves a clean cut that can be sewn up later and not leave much of a scar. However, two blades side by side leave parallel cuts side by side. These cuts cannot be sewn together without leaving very bad scarring. The person slashing with two blades together is marking his victim for life. Ham realised that the skinny ginger could be trouble.

If the gingers expected Ham's expression to change, they were to be disappointed.

"We're gonna cut you old man." Ham looked at them. Was he supposed to show fear? They were amateurs. It was sad.

"You can still walk away from this, you know. I would advise it." The older gingers were surprised. Where was the fear? The old guy should be afraid.

"What? Are you stupid or something?"

"Meow." Came the indignant reply from Ham's pocket.

"What?"

"Well, if you are sure about this." This response was not what the gingers were expecting.

From under his jacket, Ham took a Browning nine-millimetre High Power out of its holster behind his hip. All three of the gingers' jaws dropped. Showing casualness gained from experience, Ham released the magazine and pulling back the slide, checked that there was no round loaded. He released the slide on the empty chamber. He then replaced the magazine after making a show of looking at the rounds and made it safe. He stood facing the three gingers knowing that they did not know that his weapon was safe. Razors were their game.

"Ready when you are lads," Ham stated casually. He stood waiting for a few moments. They did not move; he did not think that they would. They stared at him open-mouthed. They needed more encouragement. "Oops sorry, how careless of me. I forgot something. "Ham reached behind his left hip and from another holster on his belt, retrieved a Monadnock Auto-lock Extendable Baton. With a flick of his wrists, the baton extended with a satisfyingly loud click.

"Who the fuck are you?' Fat ginger asked.

"Let's say that my gang is much bigger than yours. Huh?"

"What...?"

"Doesn't matter now does it." continued Ham. His shoulders shrugged in a manner displaying indifference. "Look, lads. I'm sure this is all a misunderstanding, and I'm sure you want to be somewhere else. Here's my suggestion and it's only a suggestion." He looked at the three who had not moved. "Walk away. Let's pretend this never happened. I was never here. You were never here. Believe me; it's better for everyone. I hate paperwork." The hint was there. It would be up to them to pick it up. They did not move. Maybe they were too dumb to bluff.

"C'mon! It's a no brainer." Gregor the ginger and skinny ginger looked at fat ginger who supposedly had the brains of the family, although that point may be debatable. He nodded almost imperceptibly. Ham casually replaced the Browning in his holster. He then pressed the button on the base of the baton, pressed the polymer tip against his belt. It shrank back to its original size, and he replaced that too into its holster. He looked up as if he were surprised to see them still there. Ham made to reach again for his automatic. That was enough. The gingers realised that they had been staring and turning walked away, slowly gathering speed to a speedy walk.

"Meow." Stated the fur-ball.

"You can say that again. Let's go home. That's enough nonsense for one night."

Getting to Know You

The next week or so passed uneventfully. Ham had taken the kitten out several times to return her to the Cat-woman. There had been no sign of the Cat-woman, so Ham bought a cat bed. He bought one large enough for her to grow-into. The kitten had decided that it was too small and had slept on Ham's bed. He would put her back in her bed, and he would wake up with the fur-ball beside him.

He bought her a litter box which she would use most of the time. When she did, she would cover the tiny piece of poo with a dune of kitty litter. In doing so, half the bathroom floor got covered as well. He bought her a scratching post when she attacked the sofa; she still preferred the sofa. He bought a plastic spray bottle. They played cowboys and Indians. If she had been armed, he would probably have lost. Gradually, they got used to each other.

Food was not a problem as the kitten happily ate everything presented and seemed satisfied with that. The kitten did examine Ham's food as if deciding on its suitability. Ham would normally prepare her meal, give it to her, prepare his own and eat it on the sofa watching TV. One time he was so engrossed in a programme, he forgot where he'd placed his sandwiches. The kitten who he still had not named had finished her meal and had made herself comfortable on his lap. Ham looked on the table, the sofa, the floor. He was sure that he had brought it through from the kitchen. Ham was confused but decided that it was not the end of the world. He wanted to go and get the food, but the kitten had fallen fast asleep. He wished he could sleep so easily. He left her for a while until hunger pangs told him that he wanted that ham and pickle sandwich. Ham gently put his hand under the kitten to lift her off his lap and found his sandwich. Lifting her off, he took his hairy meal through to the bins in the kitchen and made another.

When Ham had taken the kitten out every evening hoping to return the little beast to the Cat-woman, they had formed a habit that the kitten would accompany Ham on his walks. It just became part of the routine that he would pick her up and put her in his pocket. She seemed to sleep most of the time, although she had a strange habit of meowing at the most inopportune moments, normally when he was walking near a dog. It confused the Hell out of the dogs.

Ham did not carry his weapons. He did not think there was a need.

Visit from an Old Friend

One calm and quiet evening Ham was walking along the Largs Bay promenade when he heard footsteps gaining on him. It was not cold, so there was no need for the fast pace of someone wanting to get hurriedly home. Ham groaned to himself as he recognised the military steps. The steps accompanied by the clicking of a large dog's nails on the tarmac came nearer until they were almost beside him.

"Evening general. What brings you north of the border?" he said without turning.

"Good evening Lieutenant Colonel Hamilton. Just out for a pleasant stroll, you know."

"Retired, general. Retired! Remember, you retired me. Mentally unstable or something like that you said."

"Slight misunderstanding there Hamilton. It seems you have been enjoying an extended sabbatical."

"Really? Paid by any chance?"

"Of course not! You've been collecting your pension."

"Aaah. What a pity." Ham still had not looked at the general or his dog. "So, general. To what do I owe the pleasure of your company during my pension paid sabbatical?"

"You are needed, my boy. The Queen wants to give you another shilling and put you back on the payroll." It was only because the general was at least ten years older than Ham that it allowed him to call Ham, my boy. Ham stopped and turned to face his old boss.

"You called me crazy and shoved me out the door. Why am I even talking to you?"

"We need your particular craziness." Ham looked at the general with his bushy white moustache, and eyebrows, his penetrating grey eyes, his square shoulders and large red and blue nose fed by years of good scotch, usually someone else's.

"You don't need my craziness. You don't want to be anywhere near it."

"Why don't we walk back to your flat and we can talk over a nice scotch."

"I don't drink."

"Liar! There's a bottle of Glenfarclas in your cupboard." Ham did not say anything. He knew the message was that people like him were always under surveillance and scrutiny even when they retired or went on sabbaticals. The goons had visited to check his flat, a little bit of burglary and a lot of professional snooping. Ham turned and started to walk back towards his flat. The general and his dog followed.

After a few moments, Ham asked, "Why the dog? Cover? You don't seem the doggy type."

"I'm not, but you are. Or you are going to be." Ham opened his mouth to speak, but the confusion stopped him. He just turned his head, looked down at the dog and back up to the general.

"Government cuts old boy. We can't afford all that surveillance and stuff anymore on our ex-personnel. So, you are getting a dog. A Malinois. A retired military police dog no less. He probably has more medals than you." The general said with finality as if that explained everything.

"Are you out of your cotton-picking mind? What the Hell do I want with an effing dog, with or without bloody medals?"

"Don't say that old chap. You'll hurt its feelings. The dog's already hurt, you know. PTSD[3] or something like that from Afghanistan or was it Iraq? Anyway, he's still well capable of keeping you safe."

---

[3] Post-Traumatic Stress Disorder

"I don't need a crazy dog to keep me safe. I can look after myself."

"Yes... I read about that incident with the MacKay brothers. Nasty pieces of work there. Pulled a gun on them I hear. Can't have that. Just not done in Britain, you know. You were given your weapon for self-defence, not dealing with a couple of bully boys. If you want to go around waving weapons like that, you'll have to sign on the dotted line again old chap. Did I tell you that you've been made up to full colonel? Congratulations. That means a better pension. Here. Hold this leash." And when he did. "He's yours."

"Woah! Hold on! Are you serious? You want me to come back to work for you. You want me to take on this dog with PTSD as my bodyguard? I thought I was the one who is supposed to be crazy!"

"Meow."

"And I have a cat!"

"Good. Then you won't need to feed the dog for the first day then." The general smirked at his little joke. He smirked alone.

"Meow!"

They walked the rest of the way back to the flat in silence.

Taking the Queen's Shilling

General Maxwell stood by the window, sipping Ham's whisky. He waited until Ham had made his mug of tea and sat on the sofa.

"Great view from here. I can see why you chose this place." Maxwell sat in the armchair and took another sip and studied Ham.

"Hamish, you still have your… ah, talent?"

Ham touched the leather pouch hanging around his neck by a leather strap. "Yes, but it is kept under control."

Maxwell nodded. "Good. Good. I think we will need your skills. Something is going on in that water out there." Maxwell flipped a thumb over his shoulder.

Ham waited, but the general did not expand. He just sipped the whisky until the glass was empty. He waved it casually at Ham. Ham stood up and went to the kitchen. He returned a moment later with the bottle of fifteen years old Glenfarclas which he placed on the coffee table in front of the general.

"Are you going to sit there drinking my whisky all night, or tell me what you mean?"

"I don't want to influence your investigation. It involves some murders that have been happening in this area recently. It's no good you working on the previous cases, the local police have trampled all over our kind of evidence. Muddied the water, you might say." Maxwell chuckled to himself at his little joke, which Ham did not share. "You'll be notified if and when, and I think it will be when, the next one happens. But you need to get ready to act. I'll leave all that up to you."

"Why are we getting involved with murders? The police have that sort of thing well under control."

"Some young girls disappeared…" he paused, then continued. "All that washed up was their lungs."

"Oh, Christ, I see… To whom do I report? Where do I report? What about all the logistics? I don't even have an ID anymore." General Maxwell held up his hand to stop the onslaught of questions.

"Relax here until notified. You are on a paid sabbatical after all. Your assistant will sort out your needs tomorrow."

"My assistant? First a cat, then a dog and now an assistant. Whatever next?" Yet another smirk grew on the general's face; the general certainly liked a good smirk. Ham did not like that look. It meant trouble. The old goat was up to something, but he was damned if he knew what. The old goat stood up, straightened his clothing and stuck out his hand. The general looked down at the dog; Ham followed his glance.

"There's food in the fridge for the dog, just put in an invoice when you buy more. We put the dog basket in the bedroom next to the cat basket. There's a whole selection of other doggy stuff. You've probably seen on the kitchen table. If you look after it, the dog really will be your guardian angel. He got injured in

Afghanistan trying to save the life of his handler. Affected him a bit poor chap."

"Hold on! Hold on! Has he got steel teeth?" squawked Ham looking at the dog.

"Yes, I believe so. Jaws of steel! They are titanium or something like that. Had to be done I'm afraid. The dog's jaw did get pretty messed up out there. Take my advice, old chap. Don't upset him." The general added calmly flashing his old teeth.

"I wouldn't dream of it. What's it called?"

"Whatever you want. It's your dog."

"What's the assistant called?"

"Whatever you want. Your assistant. Hahaha. Good one what?" Ham did not smile. The general stopped laughing. "Yes, quite."

"Macduff. Captain Macduff. You'll get on fine." Somehow the general seemed to think this was funny. "Macduff is new to the department. You'll need to put on your trainer hat."

"Why me general and why now?" Ham asked.

Maxwell paused for a few moments then said. "We've lost Stevenson in Borneo and Jones in the Viet Nam Highlands. Both MIA[4]. Haven't heard from them in months, so they are down as KIA[5]. What we have left doesn't have your experience. What we have is a problem, and it needs resolving PDQ[6] That damned American, Maddox hasn't turned up yet, but you can bet your bottom dollar he will." Ham's eyes rolled.

"Is that lunatic still on the scene? I thought that they would have got rid of him by now."

---

[4] Missing In Action

[5] Killed In Action

[6] Pretty Damned Quick

"Tell captain Macduff what you need. Tell the good captain to contact Edwards, and I'll see you get what you need." He stood up, polished off his drink and made for the door. At the front door, he shook Ham's hand and left.

Ham thought about it for a moment. The old goat was up to something. Ham went into the bedroom and looked at the empty dog basket. The dog had squeezed itself into the cat basket. The cat was on the bed. Both were fast asleep.

Captain Macduff

Ham was on his second coffee of the morning when the door intercom rang. Ham's eyes flicked to the wall clock, nine o'clock. He got up and walked to the intercom.

He picked up the handset, "Hamilton."

"Colonel Hamilton. Captain Macduff. General… "Ham interrupted by pressing the key to open the door downstairs. "Name's on the door come up, Macduff."

Ham cursed fools and general Maxwell for his weird sense of humour and wondered further what other games he had in mind. It was not a good start, Macduff standing in the street, yelling out to all and sundry, names and ranks. Ham would have to have a quiet word about discretion and secrecy. As far as the general public was concerned, Ham was a doddery old nobody seeing out his retirement by the seaside, and that was the way he liked it.

Ham walked to the front door and opened it. He looked at the stairs and waited, half expecting the worst. When captain Macduff climbed the stairs, he was glad to see that at least she had not worn her uniform. Holding the door open, he invited her in. After he pointed to where she should hang her wine coloured leather jacket, he showed her down the hallway and pointed towards the kitchen. He stopped, took a couple of steps back, peered into the bedroom and looked at the dog which looked back at him from the cat basket.

"Guard dog, huh?" The dog lowered his head, and Ham returned to the kitchen.

"You have guests?" Macduff asked, nodding her head towards the hallway.

"I was just talking to the dog," Ham said without emotion. Macduff face displayed minor confusion.

"You have an envelope for me?" Ham asked. She handed over a heavy sealed envelope. He took it and continued. "You'll find tea or coffee over there." Pointing. "Milk in the fridge. I'll have tea with milk." He looked at her; she looked at him. She did not look happy. He was not in the mood for any crap.

"Look. I don't care if you are a man or woman and what rank you are. I am going to read what's in here. I want a mug of tea, from over there…" Pointing. "while I'm reading it. If you want a biscuit, they're in there." Another point. "Any problems, Captain?" A shake of the head. "Good." Ham left the room knowing that there would be some serious eye-rolling or finger flashing behind him.

"Don't feed the cat. It lies." He called over his shoulder.

The tea brought, Ham indicated the armchair to his guest. Having opened the envelope, Ham quickly read his orders and glanced through the personal file on Capt. Alison Macduff. When he'd finished, he drank from his mug of tea and stared over the lip at the young officer sat in front of him. Short blond hair framed her sun-tanned face. Deep blue eyes shone out under her fringe. Her deceptively slim physic hid a muscular frame; this was in turn hidden under a vanilla shirt tucked into a belted pair of well-fitting but not skin-hugging jeans. White socks showed on top of simple non-branded trainers completed the assemble. She wore no jewellery save for a simple man's watch. She saw him studying her and waited patiently. Most men gave her more than a second glance, but that did not mean that she enjoyed it. She controlled her expression and waited.

"Now you tell me the story. Short and sweet, please. I want your side, not what it says here." He waited while she gathered her thoughts. When she saw him reading her file, she knew it would come.

"I had been out with my team meeting an informant. He gave me some time-critical information. On the way back, the vehicle broke down. The radio also decided not to work that night. I left three men with the vehicle and came back with two. As we approached the base, a trigger-happy Guards captain decided to open-up on us injuring my corporal, so I lumped him."

"The Guards captain?" She nodded. "Why do you mention, a Guards captain? Why is that important?"

"Because he was a stuck-up little prick, without a brain in his head, who probably only got in the army because of his daddy… Sir." They stared at each other for a moment.

"And?"

"I broke his jaw." She said with a slight wrinkle of a smile.

"Quite understandable. And the problem was…?"

"His father, General Lord Bletchley, he sort of runs the army."

"So General Maxwell, thought he'd throw you to me. Interesting." He paused for a while. "Yes, I think you will do fine. Your tea is quite good. I 'lumped' a Guards officer too. They should make it an Olympic sport." His expression did not change. She did not know what to say to this old man. He looked at her surprised face. He continued. "Now to business. What do you know about us?"

"I don't know who 'us', is sir. My orders were to report to you here and present you with the envelope."

A Most Peculiar Department

"Us? Who is us?" Ham sat back and thought for a moment. He had been thinking about how to explain their job since the general had said he was getting an assistant. He still was not sure. He needed to train her, but he was not sure how much to tell her. And more importantly, how. Did she have 'skills'?

"Right! Do you have a notebook?" She nodded.

"In my jacket." Her eyes moved to the door.

"Go get it and the pen or whatever you use and bring it back here. Then make another mug of tea if you wouldn't mind." Again, that look that said, I'm not the tea-lady.

"Look." He said. "It's this way. You report to me. I report to the general and the general reports to the PM[7] The PMs not going to make the tea. The general makes lousy tea. I have work to do, so

---

[7] Prime Minister

guess who that leaves captain?" She returned a couple of minutes later with the note pad and pen which he indicated he wanted. The pad was a simple black Moleskin with lined pages. The pen was a simple Pilot with black gel. Good, thank God it was not a Hello Kitty pad. She took his empty mug and disappeared out the door. He started to write.

He paused and asked, "Who gave you your orders? Name and describe." He cocked an ear.

"A chap called Thompson. White male, mid-forties, about one seventy-four high with curly blond hair, brown eyes." She returned to the room, placed the mug of tea on the coffee table and sat down.

"Aah yes. I know the chap. It's not Thompson, but I'll let him play his cloak and dagger games. Thompson, he shall remain. Poor chap, he doesn't get out of the office much. Maxwell keeps him on a tight chain. Nearly got his partner killed the last time he was allowed out." Ham pointed his fingers at his chest. "Me… Just let me finish this list then I'll tell you what you're in, whether you like it or not." He wrote. She waited patiently. Then he looked up. "Did Aaah... Thompson gave you a secure phone?" She nodded. "Use it for any official work." She nodded again.

Ham finished writing. "Make yourself comfortable, and I will tell you a bit about what we do." Putting down the pen and pad, he sat back and steepled his fingers.

"But first, the file says you grew up in Walton-on-Thames, Surrey. That's not exactly Macduff territory, but your accent is definitely from Surrey." She nodded. He continued, "In some ways, it would have been easier if you had come from Scotland, Ireland, Wales or even the country." She looked puzzled.

"People from these areas are more likely to have grown up with folklore tales or stories of cryptids." She looked puzzled. "Have you heard of cryptozoology?" She nodded but appeared a bit unsure of herself.

"What I tell you now is the highest level of secret and some. It is so bloody secret that it doesn't have a name. You will know, I will know, the general will know, and the PM knows. I don't know who's in the department know, but don't assume that they know everything. What we know, what we do, and how we do it is our little secret. Ok?"

"But, what is it that we do?" she asked.

"We hunt creatures that don't exist. We hunt them, we find them, we protect them when possible, leave them alone if we can, and we kill them if we have to. All without the rest of the world's knowledge. MIB[8] with fairies instead of aliens."

"What about aliens?" she queried. Surprising herself, that this seemed a normal logical question to ask anyone.

"The RAF[9] deals with them."

"You mean there are aliens and UFOs[10]?" This conversation had become crazier and crazier.

[8] Men In Black a 1997 film with Will Smith and Tommy Lee Jones

[9] Royal Air Force

[10] Unidentified Flying Objects

"Dunno. That's the RAF's area of 'expertise'. Knowing the RAF, probably not. They couldn't find a spaceship at the Houston Space Centre." Ham shrugged his shoulders as if he did not care. "They look up, and we look down. We have enough of our problems. We'll leave them to theirs, right?"

"What kind of creatures are we talking about and where are they?"

"Dragons, mermaids, pixies, fairies, water-horses, not the little cute sea-horse ones, but the big ones who like to kill people, yetis, Nguoi Rung. Those sorts of things. Where? Different creatures, different places. All over. Here in Largs, there are fairies in Knock Hill over there." Ham flipped a thumb north to the hill overlooking the town.

"What!?" Her jaw was open, and she stared at him.

"I'm not crazy, Alison. That is what we deal with daily. And you must be careful that you do not go crazy. What we deal in will blow your mind. Do you think you handle it? Do you want to stay?

If you don't think you can handle it, you need to walk away. But it must be now. When we start, there is no going back."

"Too bloody right, I'll stay… Sir." In the corner of Ham's eye, there was a hint of a smile.

A Most Unusual List

Ham looked at the pad and at the list of things he had written down. He got up and left the room, returning a short while later with his Browning and the baton. "You'll need the serial numbers of these two to get them registered and get me a permit to carry concealed. On domestic flights as well." He added.

"Let's go through the rest of the list." He handed her the list and gave her a few moments to read through it. He saw her purse her lips. He thought, now she understands that this is a different world. When she finished, she looked up. He was glad to see that she was calm.

"Right. Get yourself a weapon of choice. I'm old fashioned and like the Browning. If you prefer a Glock 17 9mm, or whatever, get Thompson to sort it out. Snub-nosed ammunition, we may want the bullets to stop in what we hit. No collateral damage if we can help it."

"Silver bullets?" Her eyebrow raised as she read on.

"Yes. Get Thompson to get some couriered up from the armourer. Certain creatures are not affected by the ballistics of normal ammunition. Get some normal ammunition for human targets, but silver for when we go out 'hunting'. We'll need permits to carry concealed and on domestic flights. If we need to go international, we'll deal with that as and when." She nodded.

"IDs. We'll need them for all services. Again Thompson. Some people like to take orders from their kind. Get the equivalent of our present ranks. If we need more muscle, we'll call the general — not only the Army, Royal Navy and Royal Air Force, but also Scottish Police. If we need police IDs for the south of the border, we'll ask then. Are you aware that Scottish law is different for English and Welsh law? Let's focus here first. We'll also need MI 5[11] for here and MI 6[12] IDs should we need to go abroad. I don't

---

[11] Military Intelligence 5 or the Security Service

[12] Military Intelligence 6 or the Secret Intelligence Service

want to traipse around the country to get the weapons and IDs sorted out. I don't want to leave this area. If we have to go somewhere, make it nearby, half an hour at the most. If something happens, I want to be there before the local plods walk over our evidence. He raised his eyebrows, questioning her. She nodded.

He continued, "For the time being you need to be in this area, hotel or Airbnb, I don't mind. Do you have a car here?" she nodded. "You can use that and claim if you want, but we'll need something big enough for the dog and cat for work. I want the dog and the cat registered as military service animals or emotional support animals. The dog for me, the cat for the dog." He nearly grinned. "If we fly, they come with us, in the cabin. If the airline says no, the RAF will be carrying us. Let Thompson sort that out."

"Leave your number here. If I call, I want you here within an hour. That also goes when you are off duty. I've written my number, use it. I want you to check out the library and Google for Scottish folklore. It will give you some background but bear in mind the people who write these books don't know a damned thing. Lastly, arrange a MOD[13] courier to come and pick up these documents to return to sender. Ask Thompson where he wants them delivered. Questions?" She shook her head slowly. She still looked a little bewildered.

"Ok then, off you go and sort that lot out. Call me with any problems. Use Thompson. If something happens, I'll contact you." Ham stood up, walked over to the bureau where he opened the top drawer. He rummaged around inside and closing the drawer handed Macduff a set of keys. "See you tomorrow morning. Not too early I am on sabbatical."

---

[13] Ministry of Defense

History Repeating Itself

Professor Kristian Sandberg of Bergen University latest topic of research was the use of midget submarine warfare during the Second World War. The Japanese had used midget submarines against Hawaii, Australia, Ceylon and Madagascar, the Italians in Alexandria and Gibraltar harbours and the British against the German battleship Tirpitz in Norway. The Germans tried a few ideas but did not put much effort into developing viable mini or midget submarines. They created midget submarines types called the Molch (Salamander), Biber (Beaver) and Hecht (Pike), which although they sank a few ships during the south of France landings and around Holland were not very successful. Far more German midget submarines were lost than Allied ships sunk. Their final effort was the Seehund (Seal) which was the most successful sinking over a thousand tonnes of shipping along the English coast.

The professor's research had discovered a possible failed attempt by the Germans against the British in the River Clyde. He believed he knew where the wreck of such a machine might lie, and he and his son Aleksander sailed from Bergen in search of that wreck.

They sailed in their research ship, a converted trawler, from Bergen to Lerwick in the Shetlands to Kirkwall, in the Orkneys, down to Inverness where they passed through the locks into Loch Ness. As they sailed on the loch across Scotland they let out their side-scan sonar to test that it worked, and if they happened to find "Nessie", the Loch Ness Monster they joked, so much the better. The loch was calm, and the water reflected the mountains bordering the southern shore clearer than any mirror. It was magical.

Coming out on the west side, they sailed down through the Inner and Southern Hebrides, round the Mull of Kintyre to the Firth of Clyde. The journey took a few days, but they were in no hurry.

They were enjoying the father-son time. The weather was kind to them, and it was a most enjoyable start to their working holiday.

They anchored the boat for the night in the Isle of Cumbrae's Newton Bay next to the Eileans. In the bay, the two small islands protected the bay from any inclement seas. They took the inflatable dinghy ashore for a bite and a drink at the Royal George Hotel.

The next morning after a simple breakfast taken aboard in the warming early sun, they sailed west, past the old, dilapidated harbour crowned by the Royal George Hotel, past West Bay, through the Tan, the channel between the Greater and Lesser Cumbrae islands and round the Portachur Point. Rounding the point, they chugged up the west side of the island to just north of Skate Bay, their destination.

They would have liked to have anchored off Skate Point, but the Admiralty charts showed it and the surrounding area as a non-anchoring area. They sailed a little bit north of Eerie Point where the prohibited anchoring area border lay and dropped anchor there.

They prepared the side-scan sonar and started a search pattern over the area where the British had anti-submarine nets attached to the island that stretched across the River Clyde during the war. The computers gathered the data and stored it for future analysis. The data did show a lot of anomalies which initially excited the professor. But, he soon realised that it was probably debris from the nets or equipment left over from the submarine listening post which had been based nearby at the Hush-hush in Skate Bay. The Hush-hush had been so-called either because of the clandestine nature of the site or because of the supposed need for people nearby to be quiet so that the Royal Navy could listen for any enemy submarines in the area. Maybe it was a mixture of both. Either way, the red brick and concrete building which once held the secret was long gone, demolished and replaced with some more modern buildings.

After completing the initial search pattern, they collected their equipment and returned to the anchor point north of Eerie Point safely out of the prohibited anchoring area. After a short discussion, they agreed that Aleksander would dive down for a look. They planned that Aleksander would dive with a hookah. A hookah is a long hose, attached at one end to a diesel pump on the boat and a young fool at with a regulator in his mouth at the other.

The flow of the River Clyde was strong, Aleksander would allow the current to take him down Skate Bay, passed Skate Point and on to Little Skate Bay. Professor Sandberg would also follow the current down-stream and pick Aleksander up when he surfaced. It is usual practice for even experienced divers, to dive at least in pairs in case one diver gets into trouble. Aleksander who had been a Royal Norwegian Navy diver during his national service convinced his father that he would be safe with a life-line and air supply attached to the boat.

Aleksander went over the side and then after signalling that all was well, sank into the murky depths. Crystal clear waters the Clyde was not.

The depth varied around, but usually less than twenty-five meters. Aleksander knew that he could stay at that depth safely for twenty minutes without requiring decompression stops on the way back up. The dive was only the first reconnaissance, a quick skim of the site, so he figured twenty minutes should be more than enough time for the current to carry him over the site.

It was dark and cold, and Aleksander could not see much even with his torch. But then suddenly he did. He did, but, he could not believe what he saw. There was a mermaid right in front of him. She stayed in the beam and smiled at him; her green eyes twinkled even in the dark, her hair black flew around behind her. It was black, but there was a flash of a hint of green when it blew in and out of the torchlight. The upper part of her body, which he could see in the beam of his torch was nude. Her breasts were small and pert, capped with dark nipples.

He looked at her, and she stared at him. She was just there and then suddenly she was gone. He was shocked. He almost forgot to breathe.

The strong hands which grabbed his arms brought him back to reality. He tried to struggle, but the grip was too tight. They dragged to the surface. Only when he surfaced that he realised that he was held by two black-clad divers wearing breathing apparatus. He was hoisted none too gently aboard another boat and his diving equipment removed. It was a Royal Navy vessel, a patrol boat. He was sat on the deck looking at the dangerous end of the barrel of a machine pistol, with a stern face of a Royal Marine looking over the sights. He looked around in alarm. His father was nowhere.

Before he had a chance to take in his surroundings further, one of the frogmen who had hauled him to the surface and out of the river came over and placed a hood over his head. Aleksander started to panic and tried to get up. He was pushed back with a sharp rebuke.

After what seemed like an eternity, he heard his father's voice and heard someone moving around near him. He called out to his father and received a forcible reminder to keep quiet.

The patrol boat moved off.

Alexander was too scared to be angry. That would come later. He did not know at the time and probably never would, but the Royal Navy had just saved his life.

Going on a Cruise

Ham pressed the red end call icon on his smartphone and looked out the window for a few moments. He watched the dog-walkers and the health fanatics marching, sauntering and frolicking up and down the promenade. He dialled Macduff's number and waited a few seconds. When she answered, he told her to meet him at the Green Shutter Bistro at ten a.m. and to bring her Royal Navy and MI 5 IDs. He went to the bathroom stripped and threw his clothes into the laundry basket. He showered, towelled himself off, shaved and brushed his teeth. He gave himself a quick rub under the armpits with his Old Spice aftershave that he preferred. It may be an older man's smell, but his dad liked it, and he liked it. He was old anyway.

While he was in the bathroom, he cleared the crap from the kitty litter box. How could a cat so small produce so much poo?

In the bedroom, he dressed smartly but casually. He did not put on a tie. He hated ties and wore them only when he had to. Grabbing his Barbour jacket with attached hood, grey Kangol flat cap and Cameron tartan wool scarf, he called the beasts. The kitten came first. She went into his pocket with a meow and a purr. The dog looked around the corner first before he decided to attend. Putting a leash on the dog, he left the apartment and locked the door. Going downstairs, he exited the building and walked along the promenade giving the dog a chance to relieve himself. He decided that the cat and dog competed to see who could produce the most waste. As things stood, the kitten was probably winning. Returning from the walk, Ham continued the short distance to the Green Shutters.

Entering the bistro, he greeted the staff and ordered a black coffee and bacon roll. He took a seat where he could see the harbour and beyond out over the Clyde.

By the time Macduff arrived at ten, Ham had finished his drink and eaten his food. The dog had drunk a bowl of water supplied by the staff and eaten the dog biscuit they had given him. The cat had slept the whole time.

As Macduff was getting ready to sit down, Ham was watching past her.

"Don't make yourself comfortable we have to go." She did not look happy again. "You can have coffee when we get there."

"Where?"

"We're going on a cruise." He said, getting up.

"Wonderful. Where to?" Ham did not reply. He picked up the leash and walked over to the counter to pay his bill.

As they walked along the promenade by Fort Street, Ham suggested, "If there is not a queue, you have enough time to grab a takeaway coffee from Costas. Meet me on the harbour. Don't be late or you're swimming." She looked over and could see a patrol boat heading towards them. In that fleeting second, she had to decide, did she refuse the offer and walk to the harbour with this annoying old git, or did she rush over to the coffee shop to satisfy her caffeine addiction?

As the Royal Navy patrol boat pulled away from the harbour, she sipped her coffee and munched on her doughnut. Good choice, she thought. The dog had his face out in the wind. She looked at him. Poor thing she thought, stuck with that grumpy old so and so. Still, he looked happy, his metal teeth gleaming in the morning light. It was the first time she had seen him so since they'd met. Of the kitten, there was no sign, not even a meow.

Since stepping on board, with the perfunctory showing of their IDs and introductions, Hamilton had not spoken. He seemed to be in a world of his own.

The Master At Arms for HMNB[14] Clyde met the vessel. The crown surrounded by a wreath denoted his status as the senior non-

---

[14] Her Majesty's Naval Base

commissioned officer on the base. He oversaw discipline on the base, and God help anyone who forgot it.

The MAA saluted and greeted them, introducing himself. Ham saluted casually in return as he was not in uniform and offered his hand. They shook. Respect had been given and returned.

"What have you been told about my visit, Master?" Ham inquired.

"I am to offer you all the assistance I can. That comes straight from the admiral, Sir."

"Good. We'll only be here a few hours, I hope. There are a few people I need to see. Firstly, the officer in charge of whatever is under the water where the father and son were apprehended up. Who is that?"

"Lieutenant Commander Fischer, sir. I'll get him for you right after I have you settled."

"I'll need a room where we left alone, understand?. I'll need one of your police or do you still call them Regulators, outside, please? No messing about with Fischer Master. He comes and pronto." The MAA nodded. Ham got the feeling that the MAA was going to enjoy bringing Fischer to the meeting. Just a feeling. There was something in the body language.

"After Fischer, I'd like to speak to the Norwegian lad and then the two divers who brought the young lad Sandberg out of the water."

"The two civilians are in the custody of the MDP[15], sir."

"Ask them nicely for him. If they say no or kick up a fuss, let me know." Ham looked at the MAA and he, in turn, nodded acknowledgement. Ham knew that there would not be a problem.

"One last thing, Master. Sorry to trouble you but," Ham spoke almost apologetically, "any chance of a good navy brew. I'm dying

---

[15] Ministry of Defence Police

of thirst." The Master saw Macduff's eye's rolling and smiled knowingly. At least this strange old officer had asked politely.

The Master led the way into a quiet, nondescript building and along a corridor to a sparsely furnished office.

"I'll get one of my lads outside the door, another to bring you both a brew and I'll get Lieutenant Commander Fischer for you myself." And with that, he was off. Again, there was that look. The MAA was going to enjoy bringing Fischer to the office personally. Hamilton wondered what Fischer had done to warrant this personal attention. He sat down behind the desk and waited to see what presented itself.

What presented itself was an upset young officer, his head covered by a blond mop of unruly hair, tallish, very thin, wearing gold wire-framed glasses which seemed slightly skewwhiff and an angry expression.

"I demand to know what's going on. Why has the Master dragged me here? I have important work to do. The admiral will hear of this. Who are you?" Ham leant forward onto the desk and while still looking at the lieutenant commander, steepled his finger. Ham looked at him silently for a few moments. Fischer became uneasy.

"I am Captain Hamilton Naval Intelligence. You are wearing your hat in my office." Ham spoke firmly, but softly. He spoke gently, which made his voice appear more menacing. "May I suggest you salute or remove your hat or preferably both." The arrogance disappeared from Fischer's face. He saluted, removed his hat and put it under his arm. He stood to attention.

"Thank you, Master. I shall take it from here. You may thank the admiral for his courtesy and help this morning." Ham nodded at the Master, who with great ceremony came to attention, saluted and marched out of the room with a barely disguised grin on his face. The point made. Ham did not care how important this little prick thought he was, but there must be something interesting going on in the water near Cumbrae.

"At ease. Sit down." Ham waited until he settled, then got straight to the point. "What's going on over at Cumbrae?" Fischer's chest expanded, and Hamilton knew he was going to protest. "Let me explain something to you, Lieutenant Commander Fischer; my authority comes somewhere much higher than here, higher than the Base Commander, or the admiral. I need answers, and I need them now. No messing about."

"Sir, I cannot. I do not know your security clearance. The project is…"

"Let me explain it this way." Pause. "You are a lieutenant commander." Pause. "I will ask you once again. If you fail to answer my question, I shall send you out of the room for five minutes." Pause. "After the five minutes are up, you will return, except you will be one rank lower. I will ask you the same question again. Should you fail to answer, you will be sent out again for another five minutes of reflection. And so on, and so on."

"You can't do that!" He squawked. "An officer can only be demoted by a court-martial."

"That will be tomorrow. Today we are going to decide what rank you want to be tomorrow evening." Pause. "Now, my question lieutenant commander, what is going on under the water at Cumbrae? I'm not technical. I don't want to know the technical stuff, just a general idea."

Fischer spilt. He had verbal diarrhoea for the next half hour. He would have gone on longer and in more detail, but Ham ordered him to shut up. There was only one main point that Ham wanted clarification.

"The system that you are testing, does it affect sea creatures in any way? Does it affect dolphins, whales, any sea life? If you don't know, tell me. I need a specific honest answer."

"No, sir. This system is safer than the previous system we've used. It's better, virtually undetectable to electronic surveillance, more accurate, cheaper to run, but it was designed right from the start to be eco-friendly."

"If it's undetectable, why the panic about our Norwegian friends snooping around?"

"Not to side-scan sonar and eyeballs sir. They are physical surveillance. We can't hide from them. Not yet."

"Okay. One last thing. You say you found a second world war German midget submarine, a Seehund[16], where the nets were and that you recovered the said submarine clandestinely and have it in a tank of saltwater in a shed here? Correct?"

"Yes, sir."

"Why on earth didn't you produce it? The crew inside, two of them right, should be recovered, repatriated and buried. Some naval historians would love to get their hands on it."

"Secrecy, sir. We must retain the integrity of the test site."

---

[16] Sea Hound – A WW2 German two man midget submarine.

"Lieutenant Commander Fischer, may I strongly suggest, for suggest; read order, that you clandestinely take that submarine out of your shed and drop it in the water, say at the Tan, and quietly mention to the professor that he might want to look there. That there might be something worth finding in that new area. Say that anomalies showed up on your scans, something like that. Let those German sailors go home for God's sake! Stop playing God. Arrange it now. Got it." Ham rubbed his temples. "You may go. Dismissed."

After he'd gone, Ham turned to Macduff. "Was I too rough with him?"

"Nah, he was a right twat. He deserved it. I'd have lumped him."

"Captain, or lieutenant in the Royal Navy as you are now, you cannot go around lumping people just because they piss you off. You can only do that with Guards officers." He almost smiled. It was there at the corner of his eyes. "Right, go and arrange for young

Sandberg to appear magically in front of me. Can you also arrange for a tea for me, water for the dog and some milk for the cat? And of course, whatever you want. Please." Her eyes, only half rolled.

Mermaids and Submarines

The Master at Arms brought young Sandberg into the room. Ham invited him to sit down, and tea and biscuits offered. Aleksander looked at Hamilton with suspicion.

"Why am I here? Why are we being held by the navy? I want to speak to the Norwegian Embassy. I have…" Ham held up his hands to stop the outpouring.

"Royal Navy. We also have a Royal Navy." A little hint of uncertainty grew on young Sandberg's face. "You strayed into a prohibited area. Unfortunately, not on all maps, only the latest. You and your father will be released today. You have my word. We only ask that you take your boat back to Millport and anchor there for a couple of days. One of my colleagues thinks he may be able to help your father's research. We will know for certain in a couple of days. Please do not return to the area around Skate Bay. There is some equipment there, old but it is still restricted. Royal Navy divers are clearing the area, as we speak. You will not find German midget submarines in that area. But my good friend Lieutenant Commander Fischer thinks he may be able to help you. Ok?" Ham made to stand up but paused and rested back in his chair. "I'm sorry, how remiss of me. I should have asked you how you felt when you first came in. I understand you were suffering from hallucinations during your dive. How are you feeling now?"

Aleksander's mind overflowed with a mass of mixed emotions. He and his father would soon be free. This old guy who seemed to have some pull in the navy was saying that his father would receive some help looking for the submarine. He was elated but confused at the same time.

"Hallucinations?"

"Yes, I understand you were going on about a mermaid or something like that. Fantastic. Tell me what did you think you saw? I am fascinated."

"Well, I... erm. I saw this dark-haired female, bright green eyes, topless..." Aleksander looked at Macduff and blushed.

"Go on. I have never had anyone describe a mermaid to me before." Aleksander suddenly looked up angrily. Ham help up a placating hand. "Please do not get angry. My interest is genuine. I am attached to the Navy to study marine neural medicine. When I heard what you saw, I rushed here to talk to you. I would like to know what you saw; what you heard, felt." Aleksander closed his eyes.

"She was young, about twenty, dark hair with green tints, bright green eyes, topless. I didn't see her tail because it wasn't in the beam and she was scared away by the navy divers."

"Any sound?" A shake from Alek. "Anything else?"

"No, just that she was quite beautiful." He replied wistfully.

"That is good. You will always have that picture. Good luck with your search. I hope it all works out for you and your father."

Ham stood up and held out his hand, which Aleksander accepted. They shook hands and Alek was taken back to the MDP to await his release.

A few moment's silence then Ham asked. "Let's have another round. Tea, water, milk, and whatever you want. Yes? Right Macduff, let's have the two divers in. We'll take them together." With that, he sat back in his chair and waited.

Major

The Master arrived a few minutes before the drinks. He watched the rating place the tray on the desk, salute and leave.

"The two gentlemen you wanted to see are outside, sir."

"Thank you, Master. Do you know about the submarine Lieutenant Commander Fischer has hidden on this base?" A stiff nod from the Master indicated that he did and was not happy about it. "Make sure he deposits that submarine, and it's content intact in the Tan, that's the area between the Greater and Lesser Cumbraes, within the next few days. Should he forget and should he forget to inform Professor Sandberg, I would appreciate if you tactfully remind him. Any problems, you call me. I'll give you my number later."

The Master smiled. "Yes, sir." Ham had made a friend.

"Now let's have the two divers in. Won't take long with them, then we'll need transport back to Largs.

"Sir, I'll go and arrange that. It'll be ready. I'll send the lads in." With that, he saluted turned and walked out of the room.

Moments later two troopers entered to see a grey-bearded old man in civilian clothing behind the desk placing a bowl of water on the floor in front of a dog and a saucer of milk on the desk in front of a kitten. If they thought it strange, they did not indicate it. They marched in, stood in front of the desk and saluted. Ham nodded his head in acknowledgement.

"Thank you, gentlemen. At ease. Take a seat." The two troopers were in their combat uniform topped with the familiar green Royal Marine Commando green beret. But, instead of the usual globe and anchor, their cap badge was a dagger with two wavy lines behind it and the motto on a scroll below 'By Strength and Guile'. They were SBS[17] operators. They sat watching the cat lap, contentedly her milk.

"This, gentlemen, is a service cat, name not given yet, for this dog which has PTSD, also name not given yet. The dog is a service dog for me, also with PTSD, named Captain Hamilton. Behind you is Lieutenant Macduff, who does not have PTSD yet. It is still early days. Lieutenant Macduff and I can show you Royal Navy IDs, but we are not, understand." The marines looked puzzled. Senior officers did not normally speak this way with NCOs[18].

Hamilton saw the younger of the two stared at the dog and nudged his companion, the sergeant. The sergeant, in turn, nodded slightly.

"You seem to recognise my dog. "Ham stated in a questioning tone. "I've only recently been given my guard dog here. Do you by chance, know him?" The sergeant and corporal looked at each other for a moment.

---

[17] Special Boat Service. The RN's version of the army's SAS and the American SEALs.

[18] Non-commissioned officer

The sergeant replied, "We were in Afghanistan doing some business. Part of our troop was a dog; his handler called him 'Major'." Hamilton saw the dog react and become alert. "We got into a bit of trouble while on patrol, and his handler ended up badly injured. Major," he looked at the dog, "Major here, wouldn't leave him. The dog got pretty shot up, but nobody, but nobody was going to harm his handler. It took some time before we could get a 'Dust Off'[19]. Both were eventually CASEVACed[20] when it was over. That was the last we saw of him; but it's him, alright. The markings are the same. If he's got PTSD, I'm not surprised." There was a short pause. "Sir." Back to business.

"Right, what are your names? First names. I don't hold with formal interviews. Nothing will be written down or recorded at any time. But I do need the truth." They nodded.

---

[19] Callsign for emergency patient airlift

[20] Casualty Evacuation by air.

"Rob." Stated the sergeant and with a flick of his thumb, "Jaimie."

"What did you see when you went down to pick up young Sandberg, Rob?" The sergeant looked a Hamilton, then at the dog and back to Hamilton. He seemed to make up his mind.

"We saw the young man face to face with a mermaid sir. Weird I know, but that is what we both saw." He looked at Jaimie, who nodded his agreement. They both faced Hamilton with straight faces, defying him to laugh at them.

"Good. Describe the mermaid, please. It was female I take it?" Jaimie grinned.

"I'll say, sir. Quite a looker."

"Long dark almost black hair, with a hint of green, but that might have been the light. That's what we could see under the lad's torchlight. Bright green eyes. Almost sparkling. I've never seen eyes so bright. Cute, intelligent face. No makeup that I could see."

He shrugged. "Could only see the top of her because the darkness hid the rest. No clothes. Breasts. Average size. Not too big or too small. Dark nipples and, oh yes, no belly button."

"You are observant sergeant."

"It's part of our training to be observant sir."

"Well, you have answered two of my questions. What were you doing in this area? Can you say?"

"Just training, sir. The call came up for divers, and we were already in our gear."

"Thank you, gentlemen. That's fine. I wondered how you were so quick on the scene. As for the sighting, that will go in your never to be repeated box. Do not tell this story at any time to anyone. Not to your boss or your grandchildren in your old age. That sighting dies in this room. Agreed?"

"I don't know what you're talking about, sir. Jaimie and I know nothing." Hamilton smiled his version of a smile, a slight glint in his eyes.

"And you have told me a bit of the history of my furry friend here. He and I have scars to heal, but I think we will be fine. Unless there is anything else, that will be all. Thank you, chaps."

As they stood up, Jaimie asked, "Sir, would it be ok to talk to Major?" Hamilton nodded and waved his hand towards Major in answer, and the young corporal went and knelt by the dog. The dog wagged his tail, and the special forces operator stroked the dog lovingly.

"His name was not Major when the handler got him, but he decided that he wanted him to be called that." The sergeant offered.

"Why? Family pet name of something?"

"No, the dog became Major. Major is a damn good dog. But the handler used to release him whenever an officer was nearby. He would then go running around, shouting, 'Major! Major! Where are you, Major?' It confused the officers. Loved it." Rob chuckled and wiped a tear from his eye. He looked at Hamilton and did not see a smile. It was there; he did not know where to find it. "Maybe you had to be there, but we all found it as funny as Hell sir."

"He's got metal teeth!" the corporal called out. "Cool." The sergeant looked over and grinned.

Hamilton looked down at the dog. "I think I will be in safe hands, Rob. You can mention to your colleagues that he will be in good hands. Thank you."

The two operators sorted themselves and stood at ease in front of the desk. Hamilton came around the desk, and to their surprise, shook their hands. They came to attention, saluted and left.

"That was interesting," Macduff said as they prepared to go. "One question, sir."

"Just one?"

"Why am I here?"

"You are here to learn at the feet of the master. That'll be me by the way. You may have noticed that I am not the sprightliest of spring chickens. Groomed, tutored, if you like, by me, you will take my place. Watch and learn grasshopper. Watch and learn."

The Dog Walker

Arriving back in Largs in mid-afternoon, they had their obligatory mug of tea before taking Major for a walk along the promenade. The sun was shining, and there was a slight sea breeze. Major walked beside Ham off the leash. The kitten still without a name, was once again, fast asleep in Ham's pocket. Macduff walked beside Hamilton and wished that she had gone to the toilet before leaving the flat, but she was damned if she was going to show any weakness in front of the old git. Major sprinkled a couple of railing posts and litter bins; the gushing water did not help Macduff's situation.

"When we reach the point there are some public toilets there." He stated without emotion.

"What? How?" She spluttered. Quietly she muttered, "I give up."

"If I give you some instructions for tomorrow, do you need your notebook?"

"Try me." She said.

"We need to go to the Shetlands tomorrow morning. But I don't want to go through Glasgow Airport with guns and animals. Attract too much attention of the wrong people. Contact Thompson and arrange a Merlin from the Royal Navy to pick us up at the helicopter pad in Millport."

"Why Millport and not somewhere here? And why specifically a Merlin?" She asked puzzled.

"Millport's quieter. In, out no fuss. People wrote to the local paper recently asking why a police helicopter flew over Largs a couple of times. Millport is quieter. They'll probably think it was another emergency medical case. Why the Merlin? It's got the range and capacity. Sumburgh airport on the south of the Shetland Mainland is just over three hundred plus miles from here. An AgustaWestland AW101 Merlin can carry twenty-five fully laden hairy-arsed Royal Marine Commandos and has a range of over five hundred miles. I think she should be able to carry the four of us from here to there, don't you?" He stopped talking for a short while but then continued. "We need to arrive at the airport so that we can rent a car. One big enough for the four of us, of course. We will need a hotel room." He looked sideways out of the corner of his eyes at Macduff. She looked worried. Not a lot, but he could see it in her eyes. "You choose where you want the hotel. Lerwick should be fine. It's only for one night. I am staying with a friend, but he only has one spare room." He could sense rather than see the relaxing of her tension. "We'll fly back the next afternoon. I don't want to be away too long. If we do have to go through the terminal, we'll need the weapons and animals cleared to go through. As I said before, use Thompson. He can pull some strings. Make him feel important. Did I ever tell you the name of the Guards officer I lumped? Thompson. Great at admin, but a bloody disaster out in the field." They walked on for a while until they reached the boating pond. Macduff excused herself and did a closed-butt-cheeks quick trot to the ladies. She returned a short while later looking much relieved.

"They don't show that in the movies, do they?" She looked at him quizzingly. So, he continued. "Just when you're saying to yourself, 'I think I'll go for a pee in a few minutes', that's when the shit hits the fan, and all Hell breaks loose. Bullets and bombs are winging everywhere and are you thinking heroic deeds, no, you're thinking, God I could do with a piss." Ham chuckled, and she knew that at one time he had been in that position. Macduff realised that this was a fleeting glimpse into some of his past. It passed as quickly as it had come. He became silent for a while.

As they walked back, Hamilton commented, "We are not the only ones in the field. The weapons are not so much for the creatures as the opposition."

"Opposition?" Macduff asked.

"You don't think it's just us, did you? No, the Russians, the Chinese, The Americans are the main players, but I think most governments have at last one or two people like us. The big difference is that most of them are after the creatures to kill them. What they don't understand they kill. Isn't that always the way? The Russians, the Americans and the Chinese want to capture them to militarise them. You know the Americans used US Navy trained dolphins during the Vietnam War to attack North Vietnamese divers in the harbours. They and the Russians are still doing things with dolphins, seals, orcas and beluga whales, like using them for underwater sentry duty and to plant mines under ships. Imagine what they could do with Kelpies, Selkies, Blue-men and Sea-horses and the like?"

"What on earth are they?"

"Aha, someone has not been doing her homework. See me after class. You must read up on your folklore. Focus on water creatures and Scotland for the moment. We'll worry about the rest later."

"Sorry, sir, I'll go to the library afterwards."

Ham looked at his watch. "Too late today. It's already closed. I've got a couple of books you can have for tonight's homework, but you'll probably learn more tomorrow in the Shetlands. One last thing. Remind me to buy a ball. This dog needs a ball. Maybe one of those plastic ball picker-up and throw things."

"I know what you mean. I'll check the pet shop in town later." What time do you want me at your place tomorrow, sir?"

"I'll leave that up to you. Call me with the details tonight. Have you ever been to the Shetlands before?"

"No, sir. First time."

"Bring warm clothes." He made an involuntary shiver. "Very warm."

A Flight of Fantasy

An unmarked white Range Rover driven by a plainclothes police officer picked up Ham, Macduff and the animals and queued up to take the ferry across to Cumbrae. They were first in the queue and watched the cars of the island commuting to the mainland coming up the slipway. After the cars they watched the Millport students dragging themselves up the slope to go to the Largs Academy for their secondary education. Ham was from Millport and attended the school there when it was a primary and junior secondary school. But, he, like those destined to higher education, was shipped off to Rothesay on the island of Bute to board there in digs Sunday to Thursday. Friday after school they would travel home via Largs. The weekend was short, and on Sunday evening they would be travelling back via the ferries to their digs in Rothesay. Ham did not enjoy being away from his family and his island. But as his father had said, 'A man has got to do what a man has got to do.' He still did not enjoy it. The only good thing about Rothesay was that it had a Baths, an indoor swimming pool. He loved swimming.

They boarded the ferry when indicated to do so by the ferry staff. The short journey was uneventful. On the other side, the Range Rover went right and followed the coast road anticlockwise around the island until it reached the edge of Millport town. At the start of West Bay, they saw the Royal Navy Merlin Helicopter waiting for them on the helipad. They were on time. The helicopter had only just arrived. It was too early for eye-ballers apart from some flickering bedroom curtains. They left the car and trotted the short distance down the pathway to the waiting helicopter with its rotors still spinning idly. Even though the blades were well above them, they ducked and crouched as they ran to the aircraft. As soon as they were seated, the Merlin helicopter's rotor spun faster and took off. Next stop the Shetland Islands. Ham and Macduff accepted headsets. Hamilton spoke to the captain and after checking that Major and the cat were comfortable, promptly went to sleep.

Macduff looked out of the window watching the landscape pass below until she got bored and then she too fell asleep. Ham had put Major in a black tactical dog harness in case he needed to control him during the flight. Major, an old hand at helicopter travel settled himself and fell asleep the same time as ham. The cat never woke up.

The journey to Sumburgh airport was a couple of hours of bone-shaking noise. They woke just before they arrived with a steaming sweet cup of coffee. The aircrew gave Major some water and the cat who had finally woken up some milk. The kitten sat calmly on Hamilton's knees, cleaning herself. She too seemed perfectly content with helicopter travel.

Ham had asked that they disembark near the terminal as they wanted to rent a car there. The captain contacted the airport and arranged this.

Thanking the crew, Hamilton and the gang entered the terminal and headed towards the car rental office. When that was taken care of, they walked out to their vehicle, a grey Kia Sorento. Major sprung into the estate car's rear door and made himself comfortable. The cat, when placed in the rear compartment, fell asleep beside him. Hamilton made himself comfortable in the passenger seat, and Macduff prepared to drive. Their first destination was Macduff's hotel.

"I want you to switch off your phones, both of them please." As he spoke, he did the same thing. She looked at him but did as ordered.

"What about directions? GPS?" she queried.

"Don't worry; I know this place." He did not elaborate on this statement further.

He just said, "Follow the A970 north. You don't have much choice. We'll stop at Mackay's cafe for a decent coffee and then go to your hotel to get you checked in."

Mackay's coffee was indeed decent. When the staff looked at Major, Ham flashed his police ID, and in a stage, whisper stated that he was a police dog. He did not elaborate. Nothing more was said. Hamilton savoured his hot drink while Macduff indulged in the addition of some cake. Major half slept at Hamilton's feet while the kitten never showed herself and slept in his pocket. When they had finished, they left.

"You said you were booked at the Shetland Hotel, right?"

"Yes, why?"

"It's straight on this road the A970. It becomes Holmsgarth Road, but it's still the A970. Once you've checked in, we'll carry on north. By the way, if you need anything, there is a fair-sized Tesco on the way into Lerwick. You can grab something now or later if you need it." She shook her head.

"Not for one night. I'm fine."

"When you do go to the hotel later, I want you to be particularly wary of anyone and everyone."

"Are you trying to protect my virginity or something boss?" she asked cheekily.

"Not every guy may be a straight-forward pickup merchant. The opposition may be here too. I jest not, captain. You're playing a different game now. Pay attention to Americans. They not always our friends. There's one guy you need to know about, but I'll tell you about him later. Everyone's got a nemesis and Maddox is mine."

Arriving at the bleak-looking modern hotel, she was pleased with the warmer interior. The staff were pleasant, and the business concluded quickly. She came out of the building to find Hamilton guiding Major around checking the vehicle."

"Bombs?" she asked incredulously. "You have to be kidding."

"Trackers, transmitters, anything," Hamilton replied. It was the kitten which found the little box under the passenger seat. "As I said anything." He lobbed it casually onto the back of an open lorry as it passed.

"Let's go before they cotton on." They got in the car and drove off.

"Follow this road until we are just after Tingwall and then take the A971 west towards Walls."

Go West

They followed the winding A971 westwards bending around lochs and voes. Arriving at Bridge of Walls, they crossed over the stone bridge and kept left following the southernmost A971 towards Walls itself, or as the locals call it, Waas. As they approached Walls, the road narrowed to a single lane, dotted every so often with passing places. Driving on Shetland's single lane roads requires a certain degree of concentration, timing and distance calculation. There are local rules on how to use these passing places. Break these rules at your peril; most Shetlanders are of Viking ancestry. Ham talked about these places as they drove through Walls itself, and westwards towards the Dale of Walls. Macduff drove on, adjusting her speed to meet vehicles coming in the other direction at the passing places.

Ham pointed out that the roadside fences had disappeared and replaced with cattle grates[21] on the road. With these came the added hazard of Shetland ponies and sheep on the road. The Shetland ponies moved out of the way as the car approached, but the sheep did not give a damn. They owned the island; maybe they too were descendants of Vikings. Having demonstrated their place in the Shetland pecking order, they too moved out of the way.

The landscape was desolate. A hermit would feel lonely living in this sparsely populated land, but it had a rugged, rough beauty, especially if you hated trees. The only trees were those occasionally planted around some older buildings as windbreaks.

Occasionally, Hamilton would order Macduff to pull over. He would get out and scan behind them with binoculars. Although they had found the transmitter, he wanted to make sure that there were no cars following them. If there was, he did not spot them.

"Something's not right. I feel it." He whispered to Macduff. "Let's check the car again." They checked the car from front to back

---

[21] Aka Cattle Grids or Stock Grids – A grid of metal bars spread over a shallow hole lying across the road to stop animals from moving from one area to another along the road.

and inside out. Nothing found. "Damn it. I'm getting paranoid. Again." Macduff did not look happy, but she followed orders. She found it. She held up a small device a fraction of the size of the other transmitter. She did not say anything. Hamilton took the device and commented aloud, "Ok, we haven't found anything. It's safe to go on. Drive on Macduff." She gave him a quizzical look but did as he ordered.

They continue of eastwards through the Dale of Walls until they hit the northern route of the A971. Here they turned left towards Melby. At Melby harbour, Ham told Macduff to stop.

"Right everybody out and bring your gear." He signalled for Macduff to remain where she was. Holding his finger to his mouth, he got out and closed the door. He opened and shut the doors a couple of times and noisily walked towards the harbour. As he approached the harbour, he saw a small boat getting ready to leave. Casually walking over, he flicked the tiny transmitter onboard. As the small fishing boat chugged out, Hamilton returned to the car, telling Macduff to drive off, back the way they had come. They turned off at Norby and parked where they could see the main road but remain relatively hidden.

"We were supposed to find the first one. I'm out of practice with this bloody game." Hamilton muttered. "Hope there are no more."

A few moments later they saw two cars driving at speed towards Melby.

"Good. Maybe there aren't."

Once the two cars had driven out of sight, Hamilton waved his hand and Macduff drove off eastward on the A971. At the junction where they had joined the road earlier, they turned back to the Dale of Walls. On their return journey, they had not passed any other cars; this allayed some of Hamilton's fears; some, but some remained.

Hamilton told Macduff to turn off at a lane on their left and to follow the lane to the end. Leaving the tarmacked road, they bumped along the rough lane until they came to a white painted brick croft, or cottage, hidden from the road. Hamilton said to follow the lane behind the building and to stop.

The rear door of the croft was open, and a rotund, full-bearded older man stood with his arms around the most beautiful woman Macduff had ever seen. The vision had long brown hair, clear hazel eyes and seductive lips. At six foot plus she towered above the man in the doorway, but the way she held him showed undisguised affection. The pair smiled at Hamilton and then Macduff. They even smiled at Major and the kitten as they appeared.

The man stroked and rubbed Major who seemed happy to make the acquaintance. His amazon companion cooed and purred over the kitten, who lapped up the attention so much she stayed awake.

The Master's Master

"So, let me get this straight, young men and women have been going missing on Cumbrae over the past few months and your divers believe they saw a mermaid. Is that correct?" Ham nodded. "If that is the case, how come there has not been a hue and cry about it? I should have read about in the newspapers or seen it on the news or the internet, nothing."

"Well, we clamped down on the mermaid story. That's not going anywhere. As for the missing youths, luckily for us and unlucky for them, they were visitors, and nobody has associated them with the Cumbrae area, at least yet. They are just numbers among the thousands of generally missing at any one time." Jack Drummond, Ham and Macduff sat talking in the cosy living room. The furniture was from a bygone era, the wooden furniture was solid and worn, and the leather settee and armchairs impacted by many years of use. Drummond was at least twenty years Hamilton's senior, but his eyes, staring at Ham over a steaming cup of coffee shone clear, intelligent and focused.

"Lungs and a few entrails were found from some of the missing."

"Yes, most were traced by DNA[22] samples taken from their hotel, Airbnb or family." Confirmed Ham. "There may have been more missing that we don't know. Maybe it is not limited to Cumbrae. It could be a problem all over the Firth of Clyde, or even further."

"It smells of kelpies, but the scale is unprecedented. One or two people disappear and are supposedly taken by kelpies every fifty or a hundred years, but so many in such a short time. It is unprecedented." Drummond mused.

You don't get kelpies and mermaids in the same area." Janet added. "They don't mix. The Firth of Clyde is a kelpie area, but

---

[22] Deoxyribonucleic acid

they tend to avoid humans, have done for hundreds of years. Something has stirred them up." she stated as she walked in from the kitchen, holding a huge tray of a selection of sandwiches. She placed it on the coffee table in the middle of the room. "Help yourself." She continued placing side-plates. Pointing. "Ham, these are your favourites."

"Janet, you know more of kelpies. Please explain to Hamish and Alison about the kelpies and the misconception most people have about them." Janet Drummond sat on the large sofa with Alison and gathered her thoughts. Macduff looked at her and searched for a family resemblance but could not see one. Jack was somewhere in his eighties; white-haired, pale-skinned dotted with a few liver spots. His eyes were a clear grey-blue that showed intelligence, but they held a sadness from the life he had led. Janet, on the other hand, looked like she was in her late twenties, probably his granddaughter. Somewhere in her family line, someone must have come from elsewhere because her skin had a Mediterranean tint. Janet's hazel coloured eyes were youthful and carefree. Macduff's focus was distracted when Janet spoke.

"Kelpies are shapeshifters, who live in lochs, lakes, rivers and the sea. They can live in fresh or seawater. When they do live in the sea, they tend to live close to shore. I've never heard of them living far out to sea, but that doesn't mean that they don't. There is a lot about them that I don't know. My family tend not to associate with them." Macduff looked puzzled. Ham saw her expression and let it slide for the moment. Janet Drummond gazed into the fireplace and continued. "Kelpies live in the temperate climates, not too hot or too cold. You won't see them in the Caribbean or off the coasts of Iceland or Scandinavia, for instance. No, hold on, the Icelanders do claim to have a version of the kelpie; the Nykur." Janet paused and collected her thoughts. She continued, "Mermaids prefer the warmer climates, that's why most stories about mermaids take place in the Gulf of Mexico and the Caribbean or places like that. And yet, the most famous mermaid story takes place off Denmark. The old crest of the clan Murray has a mermaid. There is a famous story of a mermaid in the Outer Hebrides, go figure that one out. Not exactly the warmest of waters. Maybe there were some warm Summers or the stories transplanted from warmer climes, who knows. Anyway, kelpies and mermaids don't mix; usually. They are not antagonistic; they live in different areas. A bit like selkies and mermaids, they live in different areas, but they do overlap sometimes. Kelpies and selkies overlap, but their whole lifestyles are different. It does get complicated." Macduff looked as if she was out of her depth. It was unreal. A week or so ago she was a simple army officer dealing with a clearly defined enemy; now here she was in fairyland.

Seeing her confusion, Ham held up his hand and interrupted. "Sorry, Janet, but I forgot to tell Macduff about you. Please explain to her before you go on. She looks like she is drowning." Ham did not smile, but he would have if he knew how.

Janet looked at MacDuff. "Alison, I am so sorry. I thought you knew. Hamilton," Ham knew when she scolded him because she only ever called him Hamilton was when he had done something wrong. "should have told you. I thought he had. I am a selkie. Do you know what a selkie is, or who we are?" Macduff was not just drowning; she was about to go under for the third time. She certainly felt she was way out of her depth. Janet Drummond leaned across and rested a reassuring hand on Macduff's lap. Janet got up and walked across to a cupboard, returning with a glass of whisky for Macduff which she gulped down. Jack Drummond held up a hand hopefully. Janet scowled at him, and the hand quickly withdrew. Ham found the corner of the room interesting and studied it under Janet's gaze. "You, men!"

Janet sat back down and waited for Macduff to regain her composure. Macduff nodded, and Janet continued. She did so after a dark look at the two men.

"Selkies live in the sea as seals. If you saw a selkie, you would naturally assume that we were seals. But we can live on the land with earth-walkers. We remove our skin and take human form. We can replace our skin and return to seal form at will. Thirty-five years ago, I took off my skin for Jack. The general then in charge of Jack's department arranged for me to get a birth certificate so that we could be married."

"Thirty-five years ago, but you only look twenty-five.?" Macduff whispered in astonishment. "How can that be?"

"I'm a selkie. We age differently from earth-walkers. What you see is what Jack saw on the first day we met." She splayed her hands and smiled. "It only became a problem as Jack aged naturally over the years, and I more or less remained the same. That is why we live here tucked away from everyone. How could we explain to our old friends? Ham, who was Jack's mentee and of course the general are the only ones who know our secret." Macduff seemed to take in this explanation slowly.

"Do you ever return?"

"Occasionally, I will go back to visit my family. Everyone goes back to visit their family at some time, right?" Macduff nodded. "Would you like another drink?"

"No, thank you. I have to drive back to the hotel." Janet looked at Ham.

"No, we'll both stay here tonight." He looked resignedly. "After what happened with the trackers, we'll both stay here where it's safe. You have the spare bed, and I suppose I will do the gentlemanly thing and sleep on the settee."

"You are a good man, after all, Ham," laughed Janet. "I shall get you and this scoundrel here," looking at her husband, "a whisky." Ham nodded thanks, and Jack smiled at his wife as she presented them both with drinks. Janet came back with a glass of water for herself. "Whisky may be the water of life[23], but I prefer just water." She smiled.

---

[23] Aqua vitae (Latin for "water of life") Uisige beatha in Gaelic. Uisige became whisky.

Accepting that Janet was a selkie and was the most knowledgeable on matters concerning Maritime matters around the Scottish coasts, they decided at some point in the evening that Janet should join them for their investigations. Agreeing that Janet should go, Jack was adamant that he would remain as he was too old to go gallivanting around the countryside in helicopters. Suggestions were put forward for his travel by plane or ferry, but he remained firm in his stance. Janet would travel with them the next day back to Largs, where she would stay with Macduff in her two-bedroom Airbnb.

That agreed, they settled down to a pleasant evening. Janet prepared a fish pie complemented by a range of fresh home-grown vegetables.

After dinner, Ham typed out a long message on a small handheld device. Excusing himself, he put on his jacket, scarf and hat and left the building. Leaving the croft well behind, hidden in a small glen, he made his way to and carefully climbed Stourbrough Hill. As he drew near the summit, he could hear people talking. It sounded like two people complaining about the weather and wondering when their relief would turn up. Stealthily like a highland gillie or gamekeeper, he crept closer. Two men were huddled just below the crest of the hill monitoring the road below. Ham stayed and watched them for a while, long enough to hear the lookouts report in that there was no traffic on the road below. The Dale was a remote area even for the Shetlands, and any sensible person was tucked up in their nice warm home. They were speaking English with American accents, so Ham assumed that these were Maddox's men. If they were, his standard of recruitment had dropped. They could not keep their mouths shut. Ham smirked.

He silently left his hiding place and climbed down the hill and walked to a spot far enough away from the men where he could not be seen or heard. He took out the device that he had typed the message on and squirted the message into the ether using burst transmission. He waited long enough for a response before returning to the house. He told the others what he had suspected and found and what he had arranged for the next day.

Janet stated that there were some quite important things that she had not said about the kelpies and mermaids because of the distraction of telling Macduff about her background as a selkie. But because everyone was tired, she would tell them after breakfast. It would give her time to get her thoughts clearer in her head. The others went to bed, and Ham found that the old sofa had lumps and bumps in all the wrong places, made for an uncomfortable night; especially when sharing the sofa with a cat which talked in her sleep and a dog with nightmares.

"RHIP, " muttered Ham, "Rank Has Its Privileges. Ha!" Eventually, they all slept.

Two Revealed

After a breakfast of kedgeree,[24] Jack and Ham sat and talked in the living room while Janet washed the dishes and Macduff dried, Janet because she insisted and Macduff because she was the junior rank.

"You always eat fish?" Ham asked. "Must be good for Omega 3." He continued with a glint in his eye.

"Tonight, I'll have steak," Jack said in a stage whisper.

"I heard that Jack Drummond." Called Janet through the door. "The doctor said all you get is fish and veg and you know it." Jack's eyeballs raised as his head nodded in mock acceptance.

---

[24] An Indian / U.K. dish made of fish, rice, curry powder, parsley and butter or cream

"Yes, dear," he replied with a grin that said the steak was still on the menu for that night. "Hamish, I thought you had retired as well? How come you are still involved in this game?"

Ham explained about his meeting the general and his 're-enlistment', or his re-engagement after his 'sabbatical'. He explained about the dog, Major who was fast asleep at his feet and cat, still unnamed on his lap.

"You're still wearing that pouch around your neck, aren't you." It was a statement rather than a question. Ham nodded, a little bit puzzled as to his friend and one-time mentor's comment. "You should take it off. It will open your eyes."

"Maybe I don't want to see," Ham stated flatly.

"Problem is Hamish; you are missing things. Please take it off now. You can put it back on after this is all over." Ham showed reluctance. Jack indicated that he should carry on. Showing great unease, Ham slowly removed the leather necklace holding the leather pouch.

Macduff, who stood at the doorway with Janet, looked puzzled.

"The pouch contains St. John's Wort[25]. It blocks his second sight. Ham is a Boundary Walker." Janet caught Macduff's bemused expression. Janet continued, "A person with second sight can see the future, how long a person has to live, the true person or the creature inside. For instance, he would see straight away that I am a selkie." She stated this all matter-of-factly. Janet accepted this, so Macduff began to accept this also.

Ham was staring at Jack. Jack smiled back at him.

"I know Hamish, so does Janet. It is inevitable. We are human."

"I am so sorry, Jack. Of course, Janet should not leave you at this time. Unthinkable."

"Don't be stupid. We knew last night that I only have days or hours to live when we agreed last night that Janet should come with

---

[25] Fugo daemonum

you. Much as I love my wife, she cannot change anything if she stayed. She needs to go with you. Use your talent and your skills to sort this problem. You will be saving other youths. Do what you must do Hamish. Take Janet and look after her, she deserves the best. You know Alison has the gift as well, but she doesn't know it or how to use it yet. Teach Alison, guide her." Jack flipped a thumb over his shoulder towards the kitchen door and the two women. Janet looked down at Macduff, who was looking at Jack, Janet, and Ham again and again. Her jaw dropped, but nothing came out. She did not have second sight, whatever that was.

"Hamish," Jack said eventually into the pregnant pause. "look at the kitten." Ham did so, and his jaw also dropped. Macduff also looked at the cat, but she saw nothing unusual.

"Focus on the top of her head. Do you see a slight glow? Focus. She's wearing a crown. The cat is royalty." He stated. Macduff looked, and as she looked a yellow crown seemed to materialise on the kitten's head. The kitten slowly bowed her head and began to lick her backside regally. Cats are cats, after all. They all laughed. Well, those with two legs did, and Ham nearly did.

"I shall call her Princess," Ham said. They all nodded. Even Princess lifted her head, meowed and carried on licking.

A Gift Revealed

Ham and Macduff took Major for a walk making sure that they stayed well out of sight of the top of Stourbrough. Ham could now see the fear hidden inside the dog, but he decided not to explain to Macduff what he could see and how he could see it. She would find this overpowering gift soon enough.

Re-accepting his gift was a bit more than over-powering for Ham. It brought great sadness. To see that his friend was dying and that he did not have long to live; was one of the unfortunate gifts of second sight. Living with this knowledge in the past had nearly driven him crazy. It was Jack who had given him the pouch of St. John's Wort to wear. It had calmed him down, and he found that he could cope with life with the simple herb to ward off the second sight. Now that the protection was gone, he would have to cope with all that came with second sight. Not all knowledge was good, and some knowledge was painful.

When Major had had a fair run and walk, they returned to the croft. Jack called them into the sitting room, and they all sat down.

"Janet said last night that she wanted to talk about the kelpies and mermaids a bit more. We've been talking, and I think you should hear what she has to say. Janet…" He nodded to his wife.

"Kelpies are known to carry people away, especially children, but occasionally youths. Normally all that washes up on land are the lungs and a bit of entrails. Earth-walkers have assumed that the kelpies have eaten them, but that is not true. Humans breath air and to breath air; they need lungs. If they are underwater, they would not need lungs; in fact, they would drown. In the process of changing earth-walkers to creatures of the sea, such as kelpies, they must remove the lungs. I believe mermaids do the same. There is a process known to some of the elder kelpies and the mermaids which I think you might call magic. It is not magic of course but a science I cannot explain. You see this is a secret known only to kelpies and I believe merfolk. I don't know because I am a selkie. We are kin to the seals. We are mammals; we are air breathers, so we have lungs. Understand?"

"But why? Why are kelpies and possibly mermaids taking humans down into the water?"

"It takes nine months to produce a human baby. It then takes eighteen to twenty years to mature the baby to a useful youth. Remember we sea creatures not only live longer, but we also have a much longer gestation and development. In the past, when kelpies took children, those children would slowly mature as kelpies and live a long time by your standards. Maybe, and I am saying maybe, they did this because their population needed a boost. If they are taking youths, it is because they need youths now. They can't wait."

"Why? What's the rush?" asked Ham.

"I honestly don't know. We will have to find out. I have a suspicion, though. It could be because of pollution or because something external is killing the sea creatures off, or it could be a war. It could be a war between the kelpies and the merpeople. Both of those are just ideas. As I said, we would have to find out. And to find out, we will have to go to Cumbrae." Janet went silent. Everybody sat quietly thinking about what she had said. Janet stood up, smiled down at those seated.

"I am going upstairs to pack. Jack, come with me, and we can talk. Ham, you can make Alison a cup of tea. We'll be down soon. You said we leave just before two, right?" Ham nodded.

A Bit over the Top

It was just before two that they left Jack at the doorway of the house. Jack and Janet had said their goodbyes upstairs. Ham knew that Jack would not be there when and if Janet returned. Second sight was a burden.

Their car drove up the twisted lane to the main road. Turning onto the road, they headed towards the A971. As Ham had predicted, while they were still in the quiet area, the road ahead was blocked by two cars. These were the same cars that had unsuccessfully followed them the day before. Ham ordered Macduff to slow down and slowly proceed towards the roadblock. As they drew nearer, men got out of the cars. Each man totted a weapon. Ham looked at his watch. What happened next was out of his hands. He told Macduff to drive slower.

The men were in no hurry, so they waited, looking at the car and cradling their weapons. They were confident and cocky; Ham thought perhaps overly so. Ham judged that the men blocking their path were probably ex-military special forces who had gone into the private sector. They were overconfident. Their manner said prize captured; mission accomplished; back home for a bonus and beers.

The first people to realise that not everything was going according to plan was when a Merlin helicopter appeared behind to two men still on the summit of Stourbrough. The squad of Royal Marine Commandos jumping out of and spreading out, weapons raised in their direction confirmed it. They stood up and raised their hands. The marines removed the two men's weapons after a thorough search.

The next thing that went wrong with their plan was when two more Merlins appeared over the hill and descended to the road in front of the two parked cars. Some of the more alert men turned and raised their weapons to the advancing helicopters but were quickly dissuaded from any further action by the sight of the aircrew gunners backed up by a squad of Royal Marines guns pointed menacingly.

The men laid down their arms and raised their arms. The Commandos alighted from the helicopters and removed the weapons. They took the men to one side and after searching them none too gently, sat them at the side of the road.

Macduff parked the car at the side of the road at a passing spot. Everybody got out and made to the nearest helicopter. A young smiling officer with perfect teeth introduced himself and took them on board. The officer called out to a sergeant, who acknowledged and barked out his own set of orders. The other Merlin took off shortly afterwards with the remaining Roya Marines and the 'civilian's' weapons. The Americans should not have had any weapons in the U.K., so he was certain there would be no complaint. The Commandos grinning from ear to ear waved at the men as they took off. About the same time, the first helicopter took off from Stourbrough with a sniper rifle that they had found. The Royal Marines on this aircraft waved at the men on the hill as well. After all, it was only polite.

The local police would arrange the return the hire car to the airport.

Ham had not seen Maddox, but he knew that Maddox rarely got his hands dirty.

Everybody politely refused the offered Royal Navy aircrewman's offer of a brew and made themselves as comfortable as possible for their journey back to Cumbrae.

A war? Depopulation due to pollution? Or something else? Ham wondered what was going on and what he could and would do about it?

Unwelcome Dinner Guests

The journey back was uneventful as a flight in a washing machine on full rinse with an unbalanced load can be. The cat slept on Ham's knees. The dog slept at his feet. The ladies slept as best they could. For the marines on board, it was another day at the office.

Ham spent the journey pondering how to proceed. He did not want to wait for more lungs or body parts to turn up before he acted. But how could he be proactive? Having the main protagonists living underwater did cause a bit of a problem. What to do? What to do?

The journey took over two hours, but he was still not sure he had any answers when they arrived. They thanked the crew and the marines and disembarked.

The same unmarked police Range Rover met them at the helipad and brought them back to Largs. The driver was different, younger. He was not sure who his passengers were, but anyone who steps off a Royal Navy Merlin helicopter with a bunch of hairy arsed marines shaking hands and waving goodbye must be on the level. If he stayed in the force long enough, he would realise, there was level, and there was level.

They walked off the ferry, after thanking the driver for the lift and walked the short distance to Ham's flat. Having entered the apartment, Ham cast a wary eye around looking to see if there had been any uninvited guests. Macduff made teas for them without being asked, which Ham appreciated. He had intended to make the brews after his wander around the flat. Janet examined the place with a woman's critical eye of a single man's domain. It must have passed muster because she sat down without comment.

As Ham entered the living room, he observed Major making himself comfortable near Ham's favourite seat; Princess made herself comfortable on the window sill looking out over the sea and down over the humans below.

Macduff brought in the teas, and they all drank appreciatively. The Navy only believes that a cup of tea made correctly holds a teaspoon upright unaided. They sat, and they drank, and they thought.

"Plan of action?" asked Ham. They looked over their cups at him, but neither replied.

"Janet would you be willing to go in and see what you can in the waters around here? Something's going on, but I'm damned if I know what. There are too many variables. We need some knowledge. Anything." Janet looked at her rucksack, which contained her skin and back to Ham. She nodded.

"That's why I'm here." She said plainly with a slight smile.

"Captain, I want you to do some research to see if anything unusual is going on in this area, especially if it impacts the environment. Anything. You can use my laptop?" She nodded. "I have MOD encryption. Let's not advertise what we are looking at." Again, she nodded. Ham lifted a forefinger as if a thought had suddenly come to him and he wanted to make a point of it. "Get Thompson to check on Maddox. Is he still working for the Americans, or is he freelancing? Has he gone rogue? Those operative of his were not up to scratch. I would have expected better. They did not act like they used to be US special forces; they seemed un-co-ordinated, looking to each other for instructions. Yes, check on the American angle. I think our Colonel Maddox has gone private."

"Right, let's take Major for a walk before he settles in too comfortably. Major looked up at him as if to say, too late. After that, we'll go for an early meal. Agreed?" They all got up except Princess who stretched and then jumped down.

Walking along the promenade towards the boating lake, Princess decided to walk. Their pace slowed to her small steps, but they were in no hurry, so it was not a problem. Dogs showed little interest in her and those that did were warned off by a deep growl from Major. After a while, Princess got bored with walking and sat down. Ham was on the point of bending down to pick her up when Major went to her and picked her up gently in his mouth. She did not object, so Ham left them to it. The ladies exchanged glances of amazement.

Returning from their walk, Ham indicated that they should enter the Paddle Steamer, a Weatherspoon's pub. Luckily, getting a window seat overlooking the ferry terminal, they studied the menu for food and drinks. After much humming and aahing in the group, Ham went to the bar to order. Fish and chips for Janet, Steak for Macduff and Surf and Turf, steak and breaded scampi for Ham. Macduff wanted a Heineken, Ham an Abbott's Ale and Janet, water of course. Ham paid and returned with the drinks. The food was delivered later. As they ate, they would occasionally follow the regular comings and goings of the Cumbrae ferry.

Halfway through the meal, Ham suddenly said quietly but forcibly, "Captain draw your weapon and keep it under the table.

Quickly." With a slight movement, Macduff did as ordered. They continued to eat.

"Ladies, Lieutenant Colonel Hamilton, I believe we have some matters to discuss. May I sit down?" They looked up. Towering over them was a large bear of a man, pink-skinned, clean-shaven, salt and pepper haired man wearing gold-rimmed glasses. The man knew that he was an intimidating presence. Maybe he had been in the old days, but a heavy layer of fat diminished the effect. Ham looked at him and at the two heavies stood behind. Maddox made to take a seat.

"No.," said Ham firmly holding up his left hand. "I am having a meal with my friends, and you Maddox are not invited. Please go away. We have nothing to discuss." Anger flashed across Maddox's face. As his hand moved onto his chest in an obvious sign indicating that he was armed, his companions followed likewise.

"Are you threatening to shoot us, Colonel Maddox?" Ham asked in mock incredulity. "Here, in the middle of a restaurant?

Really? I mean, come on!" Maddox's face reddened. He pointed at Janet.

"She is coming with us." Maddox asserted.

"No, I don't think so. I think you should go elsewhere to play." Moving his food around his plate. "Please be a good boy and go away. I was enjoying this meal. A good meal with friends is so enjoyable; you should try it, find some friends." Maddox's hand went again to his chest. He companions stood behind, waiting for their master's instructions.

"Look, Maddox, let me make this easier for you and your babysitters. You have a Browning and a Glock pointing at your balls, excuse the language ladies, you draw that weapon you seem dying to play with, and you will find it very difficult to walk. The dog at your feet is a military attack dog, and if you look carefully, you will see that he has a mouthful of metal teeth. Nasty." If he could smile, Ham would have added a smile. Major did not smile but growled and snarled enough to show his metal fangs. Maddox looked at Major, then at Ham and Macduff and saw that each had a hand under the table. He recalled that each had a hand under the table since his arrival. Maddox fumed.

"Our weapons are licensed," Ham continued, "if I know you, Maddox, yours are not. Not here. Tsk tsk, would not look good. Is it a good idea to have Americans running around with guns threatening British subjects while they are having a quiet meal? International incident and all that." Ham knew that Maddox routinely ignored gun licencing laws in the UK and elsewhere. The law did not apply to people like Maddox, or so he thought.

"I want her to come with me," Maddox stated angrily.

"I don't give a damn what you want. It is not going to happen, understand? The bar staff are giving you strange looks, and it looks like they may call the police soon. I would bugger off if I were you." Maddox and his two apes duly 'buggered off' after scowling at Ham. That scowl alone made Ham's day.

Macduff re-holstered her Glock. Ham just brought his empty hand up onto the table.

"I would hate to play poker with you," was all she said quietly.

"That's not the end of it," said Janet. "He will be back. You did rub his face in it, you know."

"I know, but he and I go back a long way. I've worked with a lot of Americans over the years and got along fine with them, but he is the most immoral, corrupt, simple-minded person I have ever met. I am surprised that he is in active service. He is a couple of years older than me, and they haven't put him out to grass. Check on it tonight, please. He is dangerous."

"So, I take it you don't like him then?" queried Macduff with an innocent tone.

Ham looked down and continued with his meal.

Skinny Dipping

Returning to the apartment, Ham scanned the place, checking for visitors and bugs. He found no sign of either.

"It is unsafe for all of us if I stay on the land. I will return to the sea tonight. Besides I can do the most good in the water."

"Don't you want to wait until morning when it is warmer..?" Macduff smiled at herself when the others looked at her. "Of course, you are a selkie. The water temperature is not a problem. I forgot. Sorry." Macduff looked a little abashed.

"Don't be. Thank you for your concern. But as you said, I am returning to my element. I will be fine. It would be better if I go tonight. I don't know what I shall find or how long I'll need."

"I think Largs Beach on the way to the Pencil monument is the best place for you to in tonight. It is dark, secluded and sandy there.

But what about when you return?" Ham queried. It was Janet who was going out into the field, so to speak, she should say what was good for her. It was her area of expertise.

"Ok, Largs Beach it is. You take me there later tonight. I will return there at the same time when I'm ready to report or return. If I need to come back urgently, I'll appear in the water out there." She said, pointing out the window. If it's during the day, we'll meet on the island at the place you mentioned Skate Bay. That's where the Royal Navy has stuff underwater. I'll find that and wait for you. Bring my clothes. If it's during the night, I'll hang around in the water outside here. I'll know if you can see me. We'll meet at Largs Beach again. Just check every so often. If it's important, you'll have to explain to your neighbours why a naked woman, holding a fur skin, is banging on your door in the middle of the night. I think Princess will tell you, though if I am there."

That agreed, they waited until it was dark and then walked south over the Gogo Water bridge and along the promenade passed Bowencraig towards the Pencil.

Princess did not want to remain in Ham's pocket, and she declined Major's offer of carriage by mouth; instead, she meowed until Major lowered himself, and she climbed on his back. The rest of the group viewed her transport arrangement with much amusement. Major walked, and Princes lay comfortably on his back as if he were a furry magic carpet.

Ham and Macduff checked every so often that they were not followed or observed until they reached the sandy Largs Beach.

Arriving, they climbed down the short bank from the coastal path to the secluded bay. Janet took out her fur from her rucksack and took off her clothes. She was beautifully figured, with large breasts, a flat stomach and strong legs. She was unabashed by her nudity.

The transformation happened in front of their eyes, but they would find it difficult to explain what they had seen. One minute there was a naked woman with a fur skin wrapped around her, the next there a blur and a seal lying on the beach, its big black eyes looking up at them. Hamish took her clothes and shoes and put them in a diver's dry sack which he then sealed.

"Goodbye, Hamish, Alison. Take care of yourselves. I'll see you tomorrow night, or when I have some news." With that, the seal flopped ungracefully towards the water, and without looking back, it disappeared into the waves. It was a surreal moment, even for Ham. Ham recovered first and walking to the water's edge he threw the dry sack out into the water. A seal's head appeared for a moment, and the sack disappeared. Macduff looked at Ham with a puzzled expression.

"She'll secure it somewhere until she needs it. As she said, she couldn't exactly be wandering around the streets of Largs naked, just because we were not there." Macduff nodded, and they stared out over the water for a few moments. Ham felt an itch on the back of his neck. He gave the itch a scratch and the itch a thought.

After a moment's silence, Ham, Macduff and the animals returned to the apartment.

Ham had an uneasy feeling that they had been observed, but he had not detected anyone. Ham trusted his gut feelings, his itch and was not happy. A phone call to the general was in order.

A Brigadier Came a Visiting

It was mid-afternoon when the doorbell rang, not the security door intercom, but the doorbell for Ham's apartment. Occasionally this happened when a delivery person or someone like the electricity meter reader was let into the block by some other resident. Ham was not expecting any deliveries, and he had not heard the buzzer for any other apartments, so he was wary.

He signalled for Macduff to close the laptop. Everything else in the room was non-confidential, average apartment possessions.

Walking through the hallway to the door, he looked through the spy hole. Ham groaned as he observed his visitors. Trouble. He opened the door and stood squarely in the doorframe barring entrance. He waited for the main visitor to introduce himself and his guests. Ham knew who he was at least what he was, but he was damned if he was going to make it easy on him. He waited patiently, face blank as if to say yes, can I help you?

"Lieutenant Colonel Hamilton, I am Brigadier Roberts-Smythe." If he was expecting applause, it did not come. The brigadier, a tall, athletic man, dressed in a dark suit, topped with a neatly trimmed moustache and an immaculately cut head of salt and pepper coloured hair continued, "This is Captain Constantine my ADC[26] and these men are from the Royal Military Police. They were all in civilian clothing. Ham looked each in turn and then back to the general. He did not shrug his shoulders as if to say, so what, but he might as well have. His expression did not change.

The brigadier's face did though. He was not used to such insolence. His face began to redden.

"Are we going to stand here all day?" he exploded.

"Please come in brigadier and you too Constantine. It's colonel by the way, and it is retired, so the 'monkeys'[27] have no jurisdiction here. They can bugger off and get a coffee or wait in the car.

---

[26] Aide-de-campe - assistant

[27] Derogatory nickname for the Royal Military Police.

They're not coming in here, and they are not standing out there making the place look untidy." Ham stood determined to wait for the dismissal of the two RMPs. They stood stalwart until dismissed by Constantine, but Ham caught the look in their eyes as they turned to go. Hatred. Ham had no animosity towards the 'redcaps', [28] but he had to set the tone. He had to control the situation. If the redcaps came in, they would be witnesses, and the flat was too small for so many people. He stood aside for the brigadier and his ADC to enter.

He directed them to the living room, where he offered them a seat. The brigadier looked as if he was ready to give a prepared speech, so Ham started. "Would you like a cup of tea? I always make tea for my guests." Ham caught the surprised look that flashed momentarily across Macduff's face. She had wondered if he still knew where the cups were. With that, Ham turned and started to walk out of the room, not giving the brigadier time to speak.

---

[28] RMPs wear a cap with a red top

"Macduff, come and help for a moment." He called over his shoulder. Nodding to the brigadier, she followed.

Once they were in the kitchen Ham whispered, "Call Thompson, tell him Brigadier Roberts-Smythe, his ADC and two redcaps are here. Tell him Maddox got to him. He'll know what to do."

Ham and Macduff made the brews, and they carried the cups, milk and sugar through. Ham did not own a teapot, so he made it in cups for the guests, a mug for himself and Macduff. Macduff disappeared.

The brigadier was staring out of the window. "Damn fine view you have here. Prefer the countryside myself. But damn good view."

Ham sat down, and after indicating Constantine to take a cup, he picked up his mug and drank. Ham hated cups. He needed a mug of tea to gain the full benefit but serving mugs to brigadiers was not the 'done' thing. Meanwhile, the general stood and stared out to sea. Ham could see the general mentally preparing his grand speech.

Ham made himself comfortable and prepared to wait. Let the brigadier play his game. The old fool did not know the rules. Ham did.

"You may be retired, but you are still working for the army. I hear that you have been commandeering Royal Navy helicopters for your personal use, calling out the marines as your private army, you've been running around threatening members of the public in a public restaurant with weapons. The British army does not allow that kind of nonsense. It is not on! Americans, too, dammit. It could cause an international incident with our allies. What the Hell do you think you are doing man?" It took a minute for the brigadier to calm down enough to speak. Ham waited patiently. "You are to consider yourself under house arrest until further notice. I'll have you in front of a court-martial." The brigadier glared down at Ham as he sipped his tea. Ham's face looked expressionless, almost indolent. They stared at each other for a few moments. "Well, man? What have you got to say for yourself?"

"Don't let your tea get cold brigadier," Ham stated calmly pointing to the teacups. The brigadier stared at Ham in disbelief.

"Don't you understand what I have just said?" the brigadier exploded. Constantine did not know where to look. His job was to assist the brigadier, but things were not going as planned, and the brigadier was not making any headway with this man.

"What the brigadier is saying…" Ham held up his free hand to stop him.

"I know what the brigadier is trying to say, but he does not have the authority to say it. I hold the rank of colonel, but I am retired. I committed no crimes while in the army, so you and the two gentlemen from the military police have no jurisdiction. I work for Military Intelligence but not for the army. My authority comes from higher up the food chain than you and yours." He stated, looking at Roberts-Smythe. Ham took another sip. "Do drink your tea it is getting cold." The brigadier was stunned, nobody spoke like that to him. Not for a long time.

"I work for a department whose existence you are not even privy to know. It's way above your paygrade old chap. It seems you have rushed over here and tried to get yourself involved in something that is none of your business. He's played, you brigadier. We compete with the American who contacted you, Colonel Maddox or one of his sycophants probably. I don't know what they said, but I can guarantee that it is, as our American cousins would say, it's utter bullshit. I cannot explain to you what is going on because you are not read into the programme, but I will tell you this, Maddox and his men tried to kidnap a member of my party with the use of arms. What is it the Americans call it, 'Redaction'? I'm guessing that he forgot to tell you that. In the restaurant, he tried the same. The person he tried to kidnap was not only under my protection but a member of my team and critical to my investigation.

It was at this point that Macduff walked back into the room, and Constantine's handphone rang. The brigadier looked irritatedly at his ADC. Things were not going as he imagined. He thought he would get kudos for stopping a rogue officer running amok and damaging international relationships. Suddenly he was confused.

Ham's phone rang as Constantine, pale-faced, handed his phone to his senior officer.

Roberts-Smythe introduced himself. Ham could see his chest inflate with his self-importance as he spoke. Ham answered his handphone, with a simple yes. He got up and walked out of the room, leaving Roberts-Smythe to his conversation.

On Ham's phone was Thompson, telling him that General Maxwell was speaking to the Brigadier. Maxwell outranked Roberts-Smythe by several ranks, so it was mostly a one-way conversation. Even if they had been the same rank, Maxwell's authority in certain matters was higher. Roberts-Smythe was learning this the hard way.

To Thompson's question of what to do with the brigadier, Ham stated that was above his pay-scale and that he would leave that in Maxwell's hands. He did suggest, however, that Roberts-Smythe might only be 'advised of the error of his ways' as he might be useful in the future. He suggested that he might be better to have him on their side. Ham also said that he would call and report directly to Maxwell when his guests had departed. Before he terminated the call Thompson had a disturbing piece of information for Ham, Maddox was no longer working for the Americans. He seemed to have left under a cloud, but Thompson was still waiting for the exact details to be clarified. Ham re-entered his living room, to see Macduff and Constantine sitting uncomfortably on the sofa and the brigadier staring out of the window, the handphone hanging loosely in his hand.

Ham indicated that the two should go elsewhere, kitchen, bedroom, he did not care.

The brigadier stared out of the window silently. Roberts-Smythe didn't know what was going to happen to him; he knew he was out of his depths. He began to realise that Maddox had indeed played him and he did not like it at all. Somebody was going to feel his wrath, and if he could get hold of that bastard Maddox, he would make sure that effing Maddox would suffer.

"Brigadier, would you like a new cup of tea? This one must be cold." Roberts-Smythe turn suddenly, glaring at Ham.

"I don't give a damn about the bloody tea Hamilton."

"Please drink the tea, because while you drink the tea, I shall tell you what I can about Maddox. I believe he or one of his minions contacted you with their version of events. In the foreseeable future, you may want to have a chat with him, and when I find out where he is, I shall tell you." Roberts-Smythe's face softened slightly.

"That yank shit has dropped me in it." He complained as he sat down. Ham knew that the brigadier was no innocent; he had willingly allowed himself manipulated. When Maddox dangled a chance to gain brownie points with his bosses, recognition and possible promotion Roberts-Smythe had jumped at the chance. Nobody likes playing the fool, and brigadier Roberts-Smythe wanted to know how to get even.

Ham talked, giving what information he could, and although that was not much, the brigadier listened.

They left with Ham promising that when possible, Ham would notify Roberts-Smythe when and how he could help deal with Maddox.

Ham gave Macduff the evening off. She was young and needed some freedom. Once upon a time, long, long ago, Ham had been young. He understood the need for time-off. Hanging around an old guy for too long was not good for her sanity.

That evening Ham and the animals walked to Largs Beach and back. Just a man, a dog and a kitten out for an evening's stroll. Nothing was happening here.

Night Nurse

Ham awoke in the small hours of the morning knowing two things, his long-time friend and mentor Jack had passed on, and Major was suffering. For Jack, he would call the Shetland police in the morning and ask them to make a welfare check. He knew the result, but at least Jack would be discovered and his remains dealt with by the authorities. For Major, the need was more immediate.

Normally if Ham got up in the middle of the night for anything he would do so in the dark, knowing the flat he never switched on the lights, but tonight he switched on the bedside table light to find Major fast asleep but shivering, shaking and whimpering on the floor. Princess sat by his head, gently stroking him with her paw. She looked at Ham and back to Major; she appeared worried. Ham slid out of bed and joined her beside his dog. He stroked and gently patted the dog all the time, whispering soothing words.

Major whined as Ham lifted the dog's head onto his lap all the time talking gently. Major slept fitfully, his legs kicking and running, his body jerking. He was reliving the battle in Afghanistan when he and his handler were brutally injured.

Princess looked at Ham as if asking if there was anything more they could do. Ham remembered that he had been left some pills with a note saying, 'Use if the dog needs calming down. Use sparingly'. He assumed the pills were for the dog and not him. It seemed like a good time to be sparing. Ham lay Major's head softly on the floor and went and got the pills.

Sitting back down beside the troubled dog, Ham gently woke the dog from his troubled sleep. Major came to with a start, staring at Ham, at Princess and around the room. Gradually he realised where he was and calmed down. Major still looked worried. There was a sadness in the dog's eyes. The trauma would not leave him easily, so Ham decided to give him a pill. Well, that was the plan.

He lifted the dog's head and easily opened the dog's jaw. He popped the pill into the back of the dog's mouth. Job done! He took his hand away, and the pill shot out and hit the wardrobe. Ham looked at the dog, and the dog looked back. 'That ain't going in me human,' the look seemed to be saying.

Ham retrieved the pill and tried again. Major was more resistant this time, but he eventually allowed his mouth opened. Ham popped the pill in again, but this time he held Major's snout shut. Ham waited. Major's deep brown eyes looked at Ham. Major's eyebrows raised alternately, quizzically. He did not struggle. After a few minutes, Ham took his hand away. They looked at each other; then the pill hit the wardrobe again. Ham wondered if he should paint a bullseye on the wardrobe door.

Ham gave up. He got up dressed and got the animals ready to go for a walk. The walk would do all of them good. Ham wanted to think about Jack anyway, and a good walk along the promenade would do them all good.

He could always hide the pill in some food when they came back. Ham smiled inwardly at the thought.

Major knew he would try. He smiled at the thought too.

But Ham had a secret tactic; he would be 'Krafty', the pill was going in some cheese. Another smile touched Ham's eyes. Major smiled back. The game was on.

A Plan is Needed

The next morning, Major did not eat the pill. He ate the cheese but spat out the pill, several times. Major seemed happy with this result, so Ham threw the pill in the bin. He did not need the damned pill anyway.

While drinking his morning coffee, Ham telephoned the general. He did not speak to Thompson, except when the general was busy. It was not that he held any aggrievement with Thompson because of their history; it was just that he preferred to speak directly with the man that mattered. Ham talked with the general and got what he wanted. Tick. Slowly, slowly a plan took shape using the few facts known. Happy with himself, Ham decided that a celebratory walk was in order. He gathered the beasts and marched off along the promenade towards the boating pond. The sky was clear, not a cloud to see, and the air was crispy fresh. Ham walked with his jacket open and his hat in his pocket. He did not wear sunglasses. He abhorred them, even when he was visiting sunnier climes. He had seen too many posers with large glitzy shades. Not his style.

Ham was also happy to have time by himself, animals excluded. They did not talk.

Ham reached the point and leant on the railings near the boating pond and looked out over the River Clyde towards Cumbrae. The island and river filled his vision, but his mind was under the water. His mind raced with questions and theories. What was there? What was going on? He hoped that Janet was safe. Why were the kelpies and mermaids suddenly active after all these years? What had triggered them? Strange thoughts for any human. How on earth did he end up here?

Nobody grows up thinking; I think I will become a folklore investigator, I want to grow up and hunt Sasquatch, Yetis and the Blue Men. That was not part of his career plan when he became a young army officer forty-odd years ago. Sometimes the way life unfolds, is plain weird, he mused to himself. Major sat beside him, and Ham found himself stroking the dog's head absentmindedly. He looked down at Major and smiled. Major was calm, and the fear inside him was fading. Ham smiled, anybody who had known him, would have doubted their own eyes. He had not wanted the dog, but now he realised he was a good companion. He did not talk.

"Hello, Mr Ham. I see you have a new friend." The Caribbean voice broke into his thoughts. 'Shit' thought Ham. He looked up, guilty that anyone especially Cat-woman had discovered him during a moment of weakness. The smile disappeared, and he turned to look at the Cat-woman. "I take it that that bump in your pocket is the princess?" she giggled.

How did she know the kitten's name? Then he realised she was not referring to the kitten's name, but her title. Having removed the pouch around his neck in the Shetlands, he saw what he could not see before, the Cat-woman had an aura or glow about her. There was more to this woman than he had first thought.

"Why did you give me the princess? Why me?" he asked.

"I cannot think of anyone better. You are a good man Mr Hamish Hamilton. You look after the creatures. We all know you." Who's we? Ham's eyebrows furrowed. She did not seem to notice his questioning gaze. "The princess will help you." All she seemed to do was sleep, eat and poo, some help. "You are a Boundary Walker. You can see what others cannot. The creatures need you." Ham knew the benefits and perils of being a Boundary Walker, second sight, one who could see the future or see what others could not see, like the woman's aura.

"Who or what are you?" he asked as casually as he could as if it were a normal average day question.

"Why, I am a guardian." She replied as if surprised that it was not obvious. Ham looked at her. She looked at him. What else was there to say? Of course, she was. It was just another day in his strange life.

He was about to ask her to explain further, 'guardians of what exactly?' when he decided that it was better not to ask. He had more important questions on his mind.

"What's going on out there?" he asked instead, nodding to the river.

"There is great evil out there." She stated firmly. "The creatures that want to be left alone are in great danger. Someone is taking them. You will have to protect them." Ham looked a cross between puzzled and worried. "Don't worry Mr Ham; your team will help you. You are not alone. If you need my help, ask the princess." And with that, she was gone. I mean gone, disappeared, faded into nothing, as if she was not there. Ham wondered if he was losing his mind or had been dreaming. He looked around, but nobody seemed to notice.

"Meow," brought him back to the real world. He looked at the kitten which had popped its head out of his pocket and at Major who was tilting his head from one side to the other while juggling his eyebrows one after the other in the air.

"Okay, let's go home." He wondered what normal people did for fun.

A Simply Complicated Plan

During the day Ham made several phone calls. He left Macduff to her devices. It would be better if she did not know yet what he had planned. He did not have all the pieces in place in his head, but it was all coming together. He was pleased that the general gave his full support, that would make it a whole lot easier.

Princess took turns exploring the apartment that she had explored a hundred times and staring out the window at the people below. Major took turns sleeping with half an eye on Ham and sleeping with the other eye half opened, staring at Ham. If Ham moved, both eyes popped open and followed him around the room. If he left the room, the clacking of the dog's nails on the floor followed him shortly afterwards. Ham had to be careful that the bathroom door shut when he visited the toilet or else he would have an audience. And when he remembered that, he had to be careful when leaving that he did not trip over the dog which had plonked itself just outside the door. Ham tried explaining to Major that he was taking his guard dog duties too seriously, but it did not seem to help.

It was dark outside when Princess started making a fuss at the window, she meowed and talked in her way, indicating that there was something that Ham should see. He had left the blinds undrawn. Ham walked over and stared out. He had been working on his laptop, so it took a few minutes for his eyes to adjust. Then he saw her swimming about ten metres from the shore. Not seeing anybody in the area he waved casually once and turned to retrieve his mobile phone. He dialled two numbers. The second was Macduff. She answered straight away, and he told her to come straight away. She understood. Within twenty minutes, she stood in front of him. She wore dark slacks with a dark jacket; her hair tucked into a black baseball cap. A few blonde strands fell out the front onto her forehead.

"Take Major for a casual walk along to Largs Bay. Make sure you are not being followed and go down to the actual beach. Janet should be there waiting. If not give her a bit of time. I need to sort some things out. I'll see you both later." Macduff nodded and went to collect Major's leash. At the sound of the leash, Major looked at Ham, questioning him. Ham signalled for him to go. Major went. Princess sat on the windowsill and watched Ham, then she turned and looked out the window.

Macduff left the building and crossed over to the promenade. With little haste, she walked the dog, which stopped every so often to sniff a post, a wall, a seaside iron and wood seat. Even with the coloured bulbs of the illuminations strung between the lamp posts, Ham watched them as they disappeared into the darkness. He believed he saw but could not see shadowy figures follow them from the gloom. He dropped the blinds and turned into the room. Princess walked in front of him towards the door she too was also ready to go.

Macduff had given Major plenty of opportunity to mark his territory and to leave scented messages. Each time he stopped, she scanned the area around and behind them. She did not see any followers, but she felt that someone was there. If there was, they were good.

Passing Bowencraig, she walked on to Largs Beach. The tide was out, so she walked down to and across the sand. There was no sign of Janet. Macduff found a small stick and threw it a few times for Major to fetch. On about the third or fourth throw, Major stiffened and stared towards the water's edge. Macduff saw a shape flop ungainly from the water and make its way up the sand. The shape stopped and started to grow. The skin fell away, and Janet stood there naked, but her head hung down, and her arms wrapped around her body. She did not look at Macduff. Macduff realised that something was wrong and rushed forward to hold Janet. Janet muttered something about chemical clouds and feeling tired. Still naked, Janet fell into Macduff's arms. Shocked by Janet's state, Macduff did not notice Major's behaviour. He stood with his shoulders arched, his fangs bared, growling at something behind them. Then the voice spoke. The voice was calm and menacing.

"Control the dog, or it dies. Step away from the selkie." There was the mechanical click of a weapon cocked. "Now!" This time more demanding and urgent. There was a pause: followed by a longer pause. Macduff stood holding Janet. Janet was heavy. Macduff could not have let go of her, never mind stepped away from her; Janet would have collapsed to the floor if she had.

"It's alright, ma'am. You look after the er… lady, and we'll take care of these gentlemen." It was another voice. She knew the voice, but it took a few moments to register. Still holding Janet, she managed to look over her shoulder at the two figures standing behind her. She also saw the two crumpled shapes at their feet.

"Thank you, Rob. You and Jaimie, take these two down the path to your right. "ordered Ham. "You'll find a car park on the other side of the road. You'll find a van waiting there with some people who are expecting a delivery. Please drop them off then come back to help us here. We'll need some help with the lady.

With a nod to his partner, Rob hoisted one of the human forms onto his shoulder and walked up the beach towards the coastal pathway. A few steps behind, Jaimie carried a similar package. They disappeared off towards the Largs Marina.

Ham reached Macduff and Janet, and between them, they lay Janet gently on her skin. Ham believed that it would take some conscious of thought on Janet's part to transform into a seal, so he wrapped her in her skin to keep her warm. She stayed in human form. Janet was unconscious but breathing evenly. It was as if she were in a deep sleep.

"She is drugged, but stable," Ham stated.

"Does she need a doctor?" Macduff asked. Ham shook his head.

"When she was in seal form, she was still a mammal, so she has not drunk the drug in the water, she absorbed it through her skin. Let's take her back to my place."

A few minutes later, the two SBS operatives returned. Rob picked her up in his arms as if she was a small child and started up the beach. It would have taken too long to get a car. It was quicker to walk back to Ham's apartment. Macduff walked ahead to make sure there were no unwanted late-night dog walkers to ask awkward questions. The path was clear.

Rob and Jaimie swopped places every so often during the journey. They reached Ham's place without meeting anyone or attracting attention.

Tidying Up

Once upstairs, Ham asked the men to deposit Janet still wrapped in her seal skin into the bathroom. That done, he sent the two men into the kitchen with instructions to wash their hands and any area that came into contact with Janet. He told them that when they were done where to find the whisky and glasses and how much he expected them to drink. A generous glass each. They had earned it.

Ham and Macduff manhandled or in this case woman handled Janet into the shower for decontamination. Not an easy job as she was over six foot and a very well-built woman. Without comment, Macduff stripped to her bra and panties and entered the shower to wash the still unconscious Janet. After seeing her struggling with Janet's soapy dead-weight, Ham stripped to his underpants and went in with her to help wash the slippery limp rag doll form. Janet muttered something about the chemicals affecting her whole body and Ham agreed. Macduff realised what that meant, and that practicality outweighed coyness. Household shampoos and shower gels were all he had, but Ham reckoned that that should suffice. Anything stronger might damage more than help.

Ham did not feel sexually excited about being nearly naked with two beautiful naked women in a shower. In his youth, he might have considered any female's state of undress, but sadly he was way too old, and this was work. Janet needed cleaning, and that was that. He worried that if they did not quickly clean Janet's body, she might suffer aftereffects or some form of permanent damage. Best to be safe and clean her up, he reasoned. One held her up while the other soaped her up and rinsed her down. They swopped roles a couple of times until Janet's whole body was declared cleansed.

Once completed, they looked at her and then at each other. It was as if they had only just realised that they were nearly naked. Ham had a better view. He pitied Macduff, having to look at nothing better than a very old guy well passed his manly best. They briefly smiled at each other embarrassed by their situation. Ham and

Macduff then lifted Janet out of the shower and dried her off. As a seal, she could live comfortably in the cold Scottish waters, but as a human, she needed dry warmth. Between them, they put Janet in Ham's bed. It was not a case for a hospital. There were too many questions for which there were no answers. Ham believed that she was just drugged and all she needed was plenty of sleep and rest. He took that decision.

They would keep an eye on her, and if she did deteriorate in any way, he would call the service doctor from the safe house where the two captives had disappeared for interrogation. Ham did not think that would be necessary and the fewer people who knew, the better.

Ham told Macduff to take off her bra and panties when she finished and to put them in the washing machine after she showered.

Leaving Macduff to tuck Janet away for the night, Ham showered himself just in case he had become contaminated, dried and redressed. Ham put his underpants into the washing machine. Sticking his head around the bedroom door to see that all was under control he went to the living room to see that Rob and Jaimie had followed his orders and had a fair-sized whisky each in their hands. He made himself a tea and decided that Macduff could decide what she wanted after she had finished her shower. Ham guessed that she was upset with him as she had not spoken at all on the way back and only to give instructions, once they were back at his place. Ham's first wife had been a past master at the silent treatment, so he found Macduff's version mildly amusing. He also knew the best thing he could do was to keep quiet and let her fume in peace. He was guilty of using her as bait, but he had added cover for her, so he did not feel guilty. It had worked.

When she walked in a few minutes later, he asked what she wanted to drink. She said she wanted tea and Ham told her to sit down and that he would make it. She seemed mildly shocked. What was wrong with the old guy?

When he returned, she told him that she had rinsed the skin and that it was hanging in the bathroom. He nodded acknowledgement and looked around at the little group, his team. They sat around looking at him; it was time he told them what he wanted.

"Alison, I want you to go back to your place with Rob and Jaimie to get some clothes and stuff for tonight and tomorrow and return here with at least one of them." He nodded toward the men.

"Stuff?" queried Macduff.

"If you think you can find all the things you need in an old man's home, good luck to you." She smiled, sweetly and nodded.

"Have you two got somewhere to stay tonight?" he asked the operators.

"We're staying at Fergus's place," Rob replied.

"Who the Hell is Fergus?" Exploded Ham, his face suddenly dark. Jaimie looked at Rob with uncertainty on his face, and Rob held up his hands in a signal for Ham to calm down and listen.

"Fergus is a colleague, SBS, who happens to come from here, from Largs. He inherited his mother's flat. Told us he didn't know what to do with the place. When we knew we were working here, we asked for the key for his apartment. He only uses it on holidays, breaks away, that sort of thing. It's in Brisbane Street. We didn't tell him why we wanted it. We just asked to use it. He said no problem. He'd offered it a few times. Nice guy that way."

Ham humphed acknowledgement and seemed to calm down. "Okay, but no-one, but no-one…"

"Yes, boss." Rob and Jaimie said together.

"We understand." Continued Rob. "Especially after what we saw tonight. Er… boss, what did happen? I mean with the lady next door."

"'That lady' is Janet Drummond. She and her late husband are and 'were' very good friends of mine." He paused for a moment. "Janet is a selkie. Have you heard of them? Selkies?"

They shook their heads. Ham caught a glimpse of Macduff, who seemed happy to be in the know and to see others with confused faces as she imagined hers had been when she had heard.

"Selkies are seals who can shed their skin and become human or humans who can put on their seal skin and become seals. I'm not sure which. They are what is regarded as folklore creatures, like mermaids, kelpies, the blue men of Minge, Loch Ness monsters, to name but a few. That kind of stuff. Things that don't exist but do. We…" indicating Macduff and himself. "deal with these creatures. And now, you do too, at least for now."

"So, we did see a mermaid!" exclaimed Jaimie.

"Yes, you very probably did."

"Holy Shit." Muttered Jamie. "Excuse the language ma'am."

"I think Alison would be more suitable while we are working together, Jaimie."

"Macduff is a captain in Military Intelligence, and I for my sins am a colonel, but I do not want you to refer to our rank in public, best not at all. Confuses the public. I am just a doddery old man settling into retirement. Gentlemen, you may call me Ham."

"Yes, boss."

"Boss, I accept as well, but careful when you use it." Ham was learning to smile. Well, he made a good attempt at it Macduff noticed.

"Meow."

"That is Princess, and you know Major. Now, introductions over, back to your duties. You take Macduff to her place and escort her back. I'd like you to stay at her place tonight. Let me know if there are any visitors. I suspect we are up against a renegade group of ex-American special forces, what tier[29] I don't know,

---

[29] There are three tiers of U.S. Special Forces. Tier One being the highest, such as Delta Force or SEAL Team Six. Examples of Tier Two would be

probably tier two or below. They're not that good. That's only a guess mind you. Assume they are ex-tier one just in case. I've only heard a couple of them speak with American accents, but the rest could be from anywhere. Their leader, a Colonel Maddox, was the American version of myself. The difference is that he's gone rogue, gone off the reservation as our American cousins might say. I don't know what he's doing. I'm hoping that Janet can give us a clue when she recovers. Until then, we have to wait and see."

"What are our rules of engagement?" Rob asked.

"Use only such force as is necessary, up to and including lethal force if you must to protect yourself and

---

the regular SEAL units and the Army Rangers. Tier Three are larger specialist military units.

others. I don't think these guys will be following any rules of engagement. Understand?"

"Clear as day, boss."

"I've got your phone numbers. At least one of you stay at Macduff's place until I say otherwise. Okay?" A nod. "Right, you've had enough of my whisky. Off you go until I call you. Any problems, any, call me." Another nod followed by the tipping back of glasses and they went off.

Black and White Movies.

Rob returned Macduff about an hour later. He dropped her off and returned to her apartment. She had changed into fresh clothing, beige skin-tight pants and a loose green woollen top and a casual lightweight jacket. She checked that Janet was sleeping soundly and joined Ham in the living room. Ham was following his favourite pastime, watching old black and white crime movies on YouTube.

He poured her a generous whisky, and they watch the end of Charlie Chan at the Olympics, followed by Charlie Chan at the Circus. He had watched them many times before and they were a no-brainer. Good simple viewing. She drank another whisky and another and began to enjoy the show. The black and white Charlie Chan movies did not require a lot of thought. They were just what they were; simply fun.

Maybe he should have said enough and sent her off to bed, after all, she was there to look after Janet. She was getting more than slightly tipsy. But he reckoned everybody needs a mental reset every so often and a good dose of whisky was the best way for that. She had a lot to take in the past few days.

Halfway through the second movie and after her third or fourth generous whisky, she suddenly turned to him and asked what had been playing on her mind.

"How come you weren't aroused?" There was a pregnant pause. "Not a bit. Two young nubile sexy women. All soaped up in your hands, and you didn't even get a hard-on? Don't give me the age thing; a septuagenarian would have had a bone on in that situation." She looked at him seriously. Drunk, but serious.

He knew he could and should have sent her off to bed with a flea in her ear and a good rollicking the next day. Instead, he thought for a moment and told her. They were going to be working together for a while, and it would be easier to tell her to Hell with rank or position.

"I still love my wife." He replied. She squinted at him; he also had had a few drinks, so he continued. "I have been married twice. The first time, not so lucky. She never understood the demands of military life. She wrapped her car around a lamppost. Sober, but too fast. The second time I married, I was luckier, much luckier. It wasn't that army life wasn't a problem, it's a problem for every couple, but she understood and accepted it. I was away for a lot of the time, normally in Northern Ireland, but a lot of other places, even more so later when they recruited me into the MIC[30]. You should know that. MIC was and is a bitch on your married life. It will ruin your social life, and any partner you find will always know that you are holding something back. We see and do things that your average Joe cannot comprehend. You go out and hold a peace conference with fairies, you hunt and kill a vampire. How do you keep that in your head and try to have a normal relationship with your partner? My wife never knew what I did; she just accepted me as I was. I came home tired and exhausted. She just washed my

---

[30] Military Intelligence Department C. (Cryptids to those in the know.)

clothes and loved me. She was one in a million. I was lucky. Love like that only comes once in a lifetime.

"What happened?"

"Cancer. Cancer took her away. She never smoked. She never stressed. She exercised. She ate and drank healthily. But skin cancer came and took her away." Ham went silent for a while. Macduff looked at him.

"How long ago?" she asked quietly.

"Does it matter? A few years ago now. I couldn't honestly tell you. It doesn't matter. She was there and then she was not. Gone. All I had was my memories." She looked at him and realised that there was more. She waited.

"Two things, one Janet is or was the wife of my best recently late friend, you are my subordinate. I acknowledge that both of you are extraordinarily attractive. Don't get big-headed at this point. You know you are." At this point, he knew he also had too much to drink. "But I cannot think of either of you sexually. End of." He stopped. She nodded. "God, if only I were thirty years younger." He chuckled.

"Plus, I am old enough to be your grandfather. Let's get real!" They both laughed. "A final drink, then you are off to bed, and I will go to mine." He said, tapping the sofa.

"Being a boundary walker, having the second sight, caused me a lot of problems." He continued after a while. "Suzanne died and passed over, but I kept seeing her. I kept talking to her. I did not want her to go from my life. It was driving me crazy, literally crazy. It got so bad that the general let me go, he pensioned me off. Jack came to my rescue and gave me the pouch of St. John's Wort. It saved me. It blocked my sight. I may dream about my wife, I may image her, but I didn't see and talk to her like I used to." Ham was silent.

"Well, that's okay. I thought you were just gay." It was so ludicrous they laughed, and Ham filled their glasses for one last final, final time. They toasted each other and agreed never to talk about it again. Yeah, some chance!

"Do you see you wife now?" she asked after a pause. He nodded. And it was troublesome. He saw both of them. How do you go through life, having both your previous wives following your every action? Having a hard-on? Who the Hell could have a hard-on when their late wives were looking over their shoulder?

Pranksters

Ham was half awake and half-dreaming when the call came in the mid-morning. He had slept comfortably on the pull-out settee and was fighting off the need to wake up. Normally he would be on his second cup of coffee by this time, but he wanted to let his mind wander. He did not have enough facts to work out what was going on, but he wanted to try to make sense of the facts that he did have. He was not having much luck, so the call was a welcome interruption. It was General Maxwell. There had been another incident on the island.

Ham got up, quickly shaved and showered. At Sandhurst, a friend had once told him that you should shower then shave as the showering would soften the bristles. But old habits are hard to kill, and Ham never had any problems shaving, so shave and shower it was, as always.

Dressed, he put the coffee on and woke Macduff. Janet was still sleeping soundly. Indicating to Macduff that she should rise carefully so as not to wake Janet, he left to get his coffee. A few moments later, he could hear the shower. Returning to the living room, he broke down his make-shift bed and put the pillows, duvet and sheet in the storage area built into the sofa.

He telephoned the two SBS men and told them to report immediately. On the way, he wanted them to buy ferry tickets for the car, three adults and a dog. Ham was not sure if they had to pay for Major, they did not. They were to park their car in the ferry queue lane on Fort Street. If there was the time, they could have a coffee at

Ham's place. They said they had been awake for hours and had had breakfast, no coffee was necessary. They said they would be over shortly.

They did indeed arrive shortly afterwards. Ham watched them arrive. Rob got out and looked up at Ham's window. Ham pointed to the ferry on its way back to Largs and waved for him to stay there. Jaimie had got out of the car and disappeared into the ferry ticket office. By the time, Ham, Macduff and the beasts were downstairs; he was on his way back. Ham told Macduff to give Jaimie the keys to his place.

"Go upstairs and stay with Janet. No-one but no-one gets in. Understood?"

"Yes, boss." He nodded and disappeared across the street and into the red sandstone building.

They did not have long to wait for the ferry and were soon on their way across to the island.

Leaving the ferry, they again turned right and headed anti-clockwise around the island. Their destination was Skate bay. Police officers populated the site. They all seemed busy, marching to and fro in a flurry of activity. An officer waved them on, but Ham waved one of his IDs, and they parked nearby. Approaching the officer, he asked for their particulars to go down on the crime scene log. Ham declined for all of them and waved his MI 5 ID again. The officer directed them to the officer in charge and reported their absence on the crime scene log to the senior officer. She turned to face them as they approached.

Ham introduced himself as Colonel Hamilton from MI 5 and Macduff as another MI 5 officer. He did not introduce Rob as he was just the muscle. The inspector said that she had been expecting them.

The inspector was about to ask why MI 5 was involved when Ham, in his nicest voice, asked her politely to tell him what was going on. He said that he had received orders to come here by the powers that be as it was relevant to a case he was working on, but he had not received a briefing on the actual circumstances. He had been briefed by the general, but he wanted to know what the police knew. She seemed hesitant. They waited. While she decided what to do or say, she noticed Major, being held by Rob.

"The dog needs to leave the crime scene immediately." She said firmly.

"He's a police dog. He may be useful. He stays. Tell me, inspector, what crime exactly are you investigating here?" The inspector stared at Ham for a few moments before she replied.

"Possible kidnapping or murder-suicide. It's a bit unclear at this time." Ham raised an eyebrow questioningly. "Mr and Mrs Blair," a thumb was directed to an elderly couple in the background talking with a sergeant, "just arrived on the island for a day's sight-seeing. They stopped to enjoy the view and saw a naked male and a fully clothed female walk into the water and disappear. Both in their early twenties. He about six foot, or just under, dark hair, tanned skin, difficult to tell origin. The female was a few inches shorter, Caucasian, blonde streaked hair, wearing a dark red jacket, blue jeans, white and red trainers. They just walked in and did not come out. They have not reappeared again, so the Blairs called us." Ham thought for a moment. He looked around and noticed a black horse in the field on the other side of the road. The horse leaned over the short old tumbled down stone wall topped with strings of barbed wire and stared back at him.

"Inspector, I strongly believe this is related to the matter I am investigating. I would like you to listen to what I'm about to say. I'll arrange for someone to talk to your superiors to get this all agreed, but this is what I'd like you to do. Please."

"Colonel, I think you should know that there are possibly some other related matters…" She interjected.

"Yes, I know about them." He interrupted. "I believe that they too are part of my operation. When you have all the details from the Blairs, tell them that you think this part of a university prank. Tell them you've had similar cases. Skinny dipping then playing hide and seek with the tourists. Do you get the idea? Tell them not to tell the newspapers or any of the media as it will be bad for Millport's tourist industry. And then send them on their way. You won't get anything more out of them anyway. Carry on your investigation here as you see fit. We won't interfere. Do whatever it is you do, but do not enter the water. I don't want a police search team diving in this area. They won't find anything to interest them in there. I will get the Royal Navy to do that soon. There is some equipment in the water which the navy would not want anyone to see. They'll check the area and move their stuff soon. Low key."

Rob's phone rang. He muttered an excuse, stepped back out of earshot and answered the call.

"Boss its Jaimie." He called across. "You need to talk to him quickly." Ham stepped over and took the mobile phone.

"Hamilton. Yes, Jaimie?"

"Boss, we have some visitors here, at least a couple," Jaimie whispered. "They have introduced themselves as police officers and want someone to open the door. They can't see or hear me. I'm in the hallway, just around the corner. Boss, I recognise the voice of the one doing the yelling. He used to be one of us, John Paterson, but he left last year. He was a friend of Rob's. There's a lot of banging on the door, and he wants to come in. He's no copper."

"Stay quiet and stay put. Unless the men at the door have specialist equipment, the door will hold. I'll send help. Rob's on his way." Ham turned and returned to the inspector.

"Inspector, how quickly can you get armed officers to an address in Largs?"

"I'll have to check." She replied. "Why?"

"I need an armed backup for my sergeant. He's special forces. There is an attempted kidnapping going on, and I believe that they are armed."

"Sorry colonel, but this is above my level. Only the Assistant Commissioner can authorise special forces intervention."

"I can because it's my home they are trying to gain entry! The person they are trying to kidnap is under my protection. Rob is on the next ferry. If your people cannot or will not attend, he goes in alone." She nodded, and he gave her his address, telling her that if the police arrived before Rob to wait out of sight for him. But and this is a big but, no-one is to leave that building, even if they look like police officers. "Rob knows the people involved, and he'll have my keys."

"Rob, you heard me. Here take these keys. Macduff, give him your car keys. Take the car, get over to the other side quickest. Don't wait for the ferry to load up if there is a queue. Wave your ID, whatever, but do what it takes. Keep me informed. Leave Major with Macduff. Go"

"Major may come in handy. I'll take him with me." Ham did not argue; he waved them off.

"They can be there in twenty. You'd better make those phone calls now because my job is on the line." The inspector stated flatly. Ham called the general.

"Macduff go and talk to the horse but do not touch it." He did not even attempt to smile. "I'm serious." Macduff knew he was; she was getting used to his strange ways, so she complied.

"Kelpie?" she muttered quietly. He slightly nodded his head as he returned his attention to the inspector. Macduff had been doing her homework.

The police inspector thought he was mad — bloody spooks! She thought.

Ham telephoned the general to apprise him of the situation. The general said that he would make some phone calls and that he would take care of the matter from his end. He also updated Ham of the latest developments from his side. The general was also an investigator, but he did his investigating from behind a desk, where danger lurked in every file and at the end of every phone call.

Should Auld Acquaintance…

Rob was lucky in that the ferry was just about to leave as he arrived at the slipway. He was the last on board, the ramp clanged up into place and the ferry headed back to Largs. Rob waited in the car during the short journey. He bent down, unfastened the concealed compartment and retrieved an HKMP5SD; a silenced Nine mm machine pistol and magazines to complement the Glock L131A1 17, nine mm pistol he wore in a holster on his hip. He briefly got out and went to the boot of the car where he took out and donned a green assault vest. He put the extra magazines in the pockets.

When the ferry docked, he waited patiently for the other cars to exit. If he had tried to arrange to get out first, it would have confused the situation and drawn attention to himself. His turn came, and he drove up the slipway, turned right at the Main Street and right again down Bath Road. Turning right into Fort Street, he saw and pulled in behind the unmarked police vehicle. He didn't know the car, but he recognised the three helmeted figures sat waiting for him. He pulled in behind the vehicle and stepped out. A non-helmeted figure walked back from the corner to him. Rob took out his I.D. and showed it to the police sergeant, before pulling a balaclava over his head and adjusting it to cover his lower face. There were too many mobile phones with cameras around.

"Unless I hear otherwise, I believe you are in charge of this. No-one has come out since we arrived. We were nearby and got here quicker than expected." Rob nodded.

He led the way towards Ham's tenement building. The other three joined them as he passed the car. They moved quickly, hugging the wall to the street doorway. Rob popped a look through the glass and saw it was clear. He started to move to open the door.

"What about the other people in the building?" the sergeant asked.

"Leave them where they are. The tenants are safer there. There are two flats on each floor. We go into the flat on the right of the second floor as we go up. When we get to the second floor, one of you to stop anyone coming up, another to stop anyone coming down, one to the left-hand door to make sure the neighbour, if they're there, don't come out to see what's happening. You stay with me. Ok?" They all nodded. "Let's try to keep this low key. Nice and easy."

Another check through the door's window that the hallway was clear. Rob opened the door. They went in quickly and quietly. Along the corridor, and up the stairs, three looking up and the last man looking back. They went up from the ground floor to the first floor without incident. One of the policemen stayed there guarding the two doors and the lower staircase. The rest moved up. When they reached the second floor, they found the two doors shut. Rob signalled again that it was the right-hand door that they wanted. He pointed to one of the officers to stand by the left-hand door. Putting his finger over the spyhole, he signalled for the other officer to go up to the third floor and secure it. He did. Rob looked at the door;

it was intact. He squatted down and very slowly opened the letterbox. He had to push his hand in to open the inner lid. Thankfully, it did not squeak. The hallway was empty. Rob held up the door key to the sergeant who nodded. Going to the side of the door, Rob silently entered the key and slowly turned it. Key turned; he gently pushed the door. Thankfully there was no sound. He and the police sergeant looked down the corridor.

"There's light in the hallway! Someone's opened the door!" An American voice called out. It spoke with a waiver. This person was nervous. It was not a good sign. Whatever he was, he was not and had never been special forces. There was the sound of movement.

"Take her in there and don't do anything and I mean anything 'til I say." The English voice, calm and in control. It belonged to an Essex lad. Rob knew the owner of the voice.

"Back off. We have a woman here." The voice shouted.

"Is that the only way you can get a woman John? John Paterson! John, this is Rob. What the Hell are you doing, man?"

"Rob? Rob Ingram? What the Hell are you doing there? Rob, I don't know what you're doing here, but you need to back off." Rob looked at the police sergeant and shook his head from side to side. Not a good situation.

"He used to be one of mine." He whispered.

"John. I'm with the police, but I'm in control for now. How is Jaimie?"

"Jaimie! Oh shit! Wait out! He's out cold." Pause. Scraping sounds followed by a curse. "It wasn't us; we didn't touch him. She did. I got Randy to check when she let us in. Randy said that he was alive but unconscious. A bump on the head. I didn't check on his identity. I didn't realise that it was Jaimie sarge, honest. A bump on the back of his head, that's all, he'll be fine. Why are you here? Rob?"

"John, we're here to protect that woman. She's with us."

"Who's us?"

"John, I'm still at Poole with the SBS."

"Then why did she hit Jaimie?"

"Jaimie was left to guard her because she was out cold. When Jaimie took over guarding her, she was out cold, drugged. She doesn't know Jaimie from Adam. She's never met him before."

"John, listen, mate, you have to put the guns down and let the woman go. I mean it. John, stand down, mate."

"Haha, no can do buddy. It's business."

"John, you know the rules, when you leave, you cannot operate in the UK Overseas is not condoned, but they turn a blind eye. You don't operate in the UK except for the UK government."

"Rob, I'm here on official business; sanctioned. Back off Rob. Please."

"John, you've got it arse about tit mate. Sorry to tell you, but they've conned you. You're working for a Colonel Maddox, right?" Pause. Paterson was thinking. "Maddox used to; I repeat, used to work for the Americans but not anymore. He's gone rogue. He's gone solo or working for someone else; I don't know which, but he's not official John. He is not 'sanctioned' mate."

"I'm sanctioned, Rob. I am." There was a pregnant pause. Rob looked at the police sergeant. John looked at his gun. Eventually, John continued, "How do I know that you are still working for the people down in Poole[31]."

"Wait. Don't do anything. Just stay cool for a few minutes. Ok? Trust me." Without waiting for a reply,

---

[31] SBS reports to Royal Navy. SBS's HQ is at Poole, Dorset, UK.

Rob dashed downstairs and back to his car. He returned a few moments later with Major. "John?"

"Yes, still here Rob. I haven't gone anywhere." Chuckle. "Go ahead." John's voice sounded a bit less sure.

"I have a friend here. I am going to send him down. He wouldn't be here if I weren't telling the truth. Take it easy. I am going to send him down." Rob released Major and gently speaking told him to walk forward slowly. Major moved forward and cautiously turned the corner.

"Major!" John shouted. Rob could see the tip of the dog's tail as it wagged. "How? How come he's here? How are you, boy? My God, the last time I saw you. Holy Shit! Cool teeth!"

"They patched him up, John. He's still in service. He works for the owner of this flat. John put the gun down and let us talk face to face. I'm still in charge here, and there's no harm done. I can help you mate. John, give me a chance to fix this. Trust me, John."

There was another pause, and then the scraping sound as the pistol slid out into the hallway.

"What about the other guy? Randy, you called him."

"Randy, leave the woman and bring your pistol out here."

"But the boss…"

"Randy, I said I would look after you, right? Trust me on this one. If you want to walk away from this. Bring the gun out here. Randy, now!" A muffled groan and moan and the sound of a few steps. The colonel had some squeaky floorboards that needed fixing. Another pistol slid out into view. Rob nodded to the police sergeant, and they moved carefully forward. Around the corner, both John and Randy stood with their arms raised. John stood dressed in a police sergeant's uniform and Randy in a PC's[32].

After a thorough search, and their arms were allowed down.

"Never thought I'd see you in a monkey suit," Rob commented.

"Oy!" The police sergeant called out.

"Sorry. Slipped out." Rob grinned sideways at Paterson.

---

[32] Police Constable

They were moved into the living room and told to sit. The sergeant stood guard over them, his machine pistol pointing purposefully in their direction. Rob may have seemingly forgiven them, but the police sergeant had not.

Rob quickly checked Jaimie and decided that he would live. He had a thick skull, no dents, no blood or liquid from his ears. He was not snoring and had worse happen to him. Maybe he would have a bit of concussion when he woke up, but Rob doubted it, the lad had a head like a rock. Lying him in the recovery position Rob then went into the bedroom where he found Janet sat on the bed with her face in her hands. She wore brown trousers and a yellow shirt. A grey pullover lay on the bed beside her.

"You ok ma'am?" He asked. She nodded, taking her hands away from a tearful face. Tearful women never looked pretty Rob thought.

"I could hear. The men kept shouting 'Police, open up'. It woke me up. I thought your friend was the intruder and those men were the police. I hit him with a torch." Rob had seen it on the floor in the hallway. Although his mind told him that it was out of place, it was not enough to register a query at the time. What on Earth was the colonel doing with a large foot long black metal Mag-Lite in his bedroom?

"If you feel up to it, would you make everyone a coffee? I think we could all do with one. I would do it, but I have to report back to the colonel." She nodded and left to go to the kitchen. It would give her something to do, take her mind off her unfortunate mistake.

Rob went into the living room and asked the sergeant to stand-down his men and to bring them into the living room. When they came, one of the policemen offered to tend to Jaimie. Rob shook his head.

"He's a marine. He's got a skull like a brick, stick a cushion under his head, and he'll be fine. With Jaimie lying comfortably on the hall floor, Janet having made the refreshments decided to play nursemaid to her victim. Rob excused himself and went into the bedroom to call the colonel.

The general had worked his magic once again. The police drank their coffee, and with Rob and Janet's thanks, they left probably to have a coffee somewhere else. Some gentlemen arrived about twenty minutes later to take John and Randy away to a safe house for interrogation. Rob knew that the inquisitors were thorough. It would not be pleasant for John and Randy. The colonel said that there would be no charges if they co-operate fully. Fully meant everything and the inquisitors would make sure that they squeezed everything out of them.

As John left in handcuffs with the interrogation team's heavies, he stopped and looked earnestly at Rob.

"Thanks, mate. Things could have gone really bad today. I think if it had been anyone else, it would have been a different story."

He smiled at Jaimie who had now recovered and quipped with false bravado, "A woman, huh? You got knocked out by a woman. The service isn't what it used to be." He tutted and left, smiling at his little joke. Jaimie gave him the finger.

"What do we do now?" Janet asked.

"We wait for the boss to make an appearance," Rob replied, getting up. "Do you fancy another cup? No, no corporal, you rest, your sergeant will get your brew." Jaimie leaned back on the sofa and Janet tutted her disapproval. Rob grinned as he walked out to the kitchen. It had gone well. He thought he was going to have to kill John. He would have, but he was glad that he did not. Maybe John would wish he had when the interrogators had finished with him.

Straight from the Horse's Mouth

Finishing his phone call with the general, Ham walked over to Macduff who was having a one-way conversation with the black horse. As he approached, she looked over at him and raised her eyebrows in a questioning manner.

Ham looked at her and the horse. The horse looked at him and Macduff. Macduff looked at Ham, the horse and the heavens.

"I am Hamish Hamilton. I am a boundary walker." He looked at the kelpie in horse form to see if it understood. He decided that he could not tell. "I have been sent with my assistant to investigate what is going on here. What can you tell me?" Ham looked at the horse, which did not reply. It was not going to be easy.

"As a boundary walker or one who has the second sight, I can see you for what you are. I know what you are. Do you understand me?" The horse looked at the pair of them and then across at the police officers.

"What do you want to know boundary walker?" the horse muttered softly.

"Why are your people, the kelpies, taking people into the water?" There was a pause as the kelpie pondered the answer.

"Your people are taking our people away. Without enough of our people to breed, we will die away. We need fresh blood. Already so many die from the pollution you pour and throw into our water. My people cannot live with the vibration and noise of your craft."

"Do you kill our people for their blood?" Ham asked horrified.

"No, no. We only eat seaweed and plant life. We do not eat fish or any living creature in the water. We are peaceful; we do not kill. We are not like you."

"Then what happens to the people you take into the water?" Macduff asked.

"They become us. You take our people away; we take yours to replace them." There was a silence for a while. All three looked at each other.

"I won't ask how, but why do you remove the humans' lungs?" Ham queried.

"You cannot breathe with lungs underwater." Came the simple reply.

"Can they come back?" he asked.

"Yes for a short time, but they don't want to. Your people become our people, and they are happy."

"How come you are breathing on land then?"

"We can all come out of the water for a while, but we must return."

"You said your people were taken away, by my people, where, and how?"

"They were put to sleep and carried away to the valley of the dead iron fish. The crafts that hold people underwater." 'Submarines' thought Ham.

"How were they put to sleep and carried away?"

"An iron fish came to our water, and the water changed. We all slept. When we woke, some of my people were missing. One time I was on the other side of the island. I returned as men with black skin from the iron fish carried some of my people back to the craft. We are a peaceful people; I could do nothing. They took them. I followed. They swam to the island in the valley of the dead iron fish. There is a hole in the island, underwater. Their fish craft swims in there. I dare not follow. It smelt evil."

"Who decided to take humans into the water? Who made the decision?" Ham asked.

"We all did. We always do. When you kill one of us, we take one of yours. We always have." It was said so innocently that Ham immediately believed it. People had always thought that the kelpies had taken humans to kill and eat, but they were replenishing their breeding stock. An eye for an eye in very basic terms.

"Will you help us to find out what is happening to your people." The horse nodded. "How long will it take to get to the valley of dead iron fish?"

" I could swim there and back before darkness comes." After a short pause, Ham thought, 'I don't have a clue how fast a kelpie swims'.

"Tomorrow, as darkness comes, I will return in a small craft. Will you show me the island?"

"You should go now as the female over there is looking strangely at you." Ham knew that the horse meant the police inspector.

"I am going to stroke you, as people would a horse. I do not want to go into the water. Do not attempt to take me with you." The horse nodded and whinnied.

Ham petted and stroked the horse for a few minutes while muttering a few pleasant horsey statements out loud for the inspector.

When he thought that he had done that enough, Ham led Macduff over to the inspector.

"Could we have one of your chaps drive us to the ferry, please. We can walk if they're all busy, it's not far."

"Gordon, take them to the ferry please," the inspector called to one of the officers.

"Did the horse tell you anything?" she asked sarcastically.

"Said you were doing a marvellous job," replied Ham sweetly.

As the car drove off, the inspector muttered, "Bloody spooks."

THE HOMECOMING

On the ferry back to Largs Ham excused himself saying that he had to report back to the general. The traffic on the ferry was light, so Ham easily found a quiet spot for his phone call. He had been thinking since talking with the horse and did not want anyone to overhear his conversation.

He explained to the general where he was and what had happened both on Cumbrae and in Largs and what was on his mind. The general asked a few questions and said that he would do what he could from his end. He also agreed that they would talk later that evening. Ham thanked him and said that he would have a better idea of what was going on and would update the general once he had debriefed the team in Largs. That would also give him time to think through planning for the operation and logistics for his plan. The plan that was forming in his head was complex and a bit daunting.

When the ferry berthed, they walked immediately to Ham's apartment. Setting his priorities, Ham asked for a mug of tea and asked Janet to join him for a quiet chat in his bedroom.

Janet explained that she had found the kelpie habitat and that the kelpies were behaving in their normal manner; relaxing, playing, harvesting seaweed and other aquatic plants. She said they did not appear aggressive or agitated. Times in the past when she had come across a colony of kelpies off the Shetlands they had behaved in much the same way. She could not communicate with them as she did not understand the kelpie underwater language.

It was in the evening when she had indicated that she was ready to come ashore that she heard a strange noise in the water. It was mechanical, but she could not see any boats or ships on the surface. She was diving down to investigate further when she suddenly became very drowsy and had difficulty focussing on her surroundings. Realising that she must make it to the shore or drown, she fought the tiredness and confusion. With the last of her willpower, she made it to the beach, where she finally gave in and collapsed.

The next thing she knew, she awoke to find herself lying in Ham's bed and the police shouting for the door to be opened. She looked around the bedroom door to see a strange man, who she now knows to be Jaimie peeking around the corner towards the front door holding a gun. Believing that this man had somehow kidnapped her, she looked around for a weapon. She found Ham's large black Maglite and proceeded to lay the man out cold.

She let the policemen into the flat, forgetting that she was still naked. It was only then that she realised that they were not behaving like police officers and that she might have made a mistake. They seemed more interested in getting her dressed and away. When Rob and the real police turned up, it was too late. They were trapped. They never harmed or threatened her. She hoped that she had not hurt or injured Jaimie.

Ham assured her that she had not, or Rob would have made sure that he would be in a hospital already.

Next, he asked Jaimie to come into the bedroom for a quiet chat. Jaimie explained that all was quiet until the police turned up at the door. Jaimie said that he was not going to let anyone in and besides, he did not believe they were police officers. What clinched it for him was hearing John Paterson's voice. They had spent a lot of time together in the SBS and Jaimie knew his voice. John had told them tales about his life before joining the marines; he had been a bit of a lad, and nobody thought the police would have accepted him.

Ham asked him how his head was and got an apologetic grin in reply. "Sorry about that boss, I forgot to watch my six."

The next to enter the room was Rob. Rob explained what had happened since he had left the island. He explained that he was glad that it had ended peacefully but emphasised that he would have dealt with him if it came to it.

Ham thanked Rob for his report. He said that he needed a bit of time to think. He asked Rob to make him a brew. He also said that he wanted to talk further with Rob later and that they would use the pretext that they needed some shopping. He and Rob would walk to Morrison's supermarket.

A PRIVATE SHOPPING TRIP

Asking the others to remain with Major and the princess, Ham said that he and Rob were off to replenish his food and drink supplies, five adults and two pets depleted the cupboard and fridge at an alarming rate. Macduff had offered to drive so that they did not need to carry the supplies, but Ham said that both he and Rob needed the exercise. Jaimie had started to offer to come with them but stopped when Rob gave him the 'look'. Janet had asked them to bring plenty of fish; the fresher, the better. Macduff watched them depart with suspicion in her eyes.

During the walk along Gogo Street to the railway crossing and then on to Morrison's, Ham had outlined his expectations and plans for the forthcoming operation.

Ham knew what they needed to do and had some ideas about how and what was needed, but Ham bowed to Rob's experience in his area of expertise, especially in special forces tactics and equipment.

Ham explained that he thought he knew the place that the kelpie called the 'graveyard of the iron fish'. The Rockall Trough was a deep gouge in the Atlantic floor that ran south to north along the west coast of Eire and western Scotland. In the area north of Eire and Northern Ireland and west of Scotland, there lay many World War Two German U-boats or submarines. As many convoys going between America to Liverpool and Glasgow during the war had to pass through this area, it was a favourite hunting ground for the Germans, especially at the beginning of the war. It was also a favourite hunting ground for the Royal Navy ships and RAF aircraft hunting the submarines. The success of the hunters hunting the hunters forced the Germans further out into the Atlantic.

Rockall which gave its name to the trough is a barren granite rock sticking up a proud seventeen meters out in the middle of nowhere. It covers a mere four hundred and eighty-four meters square and most of that is vertical cliffs. In 1971 the British Admiralty under the code name of Operation Top Hat, a light beacon was installed to warn shipping of its existence. There were other small islands nearer to the Scottish coast. Ham believed he knew which of these islands held the secret of the kelpies.

They arrived at Morrison's still discussing the plan, so they found a quiet corner in the café and drank a coffee and continued their discussion in hushed tones.

Rob told Ham what he thought they needed and Ham agreed to most and said that he would discuss the matter with the general. They did disagree on one matter. Ham insisted that the operation remained within their group, Rob wanted more operators from the SBS brought in, but Ham was adamant; there were already too many people involved. Ham stated that he believed that they would find the captured kelpies and the knowledge of their existence could not be shared. Ham did say that he had an idea how to get around that problem and that they would discuss it after he had talked to the general. The general was, 'he who decides all'.

Having finished their discussion and coffee, they shopped for the supplies and returned to the flat. Rob complained that he had the heavier load and Ham reminded him with the hint of a smile, that age and rank had its privileges.

Arriving back at the flat, Rob excused himself and left. Ham asked Jaimie to remain as he wanted him to stay behind and guard Janet when Ham went for his evening walk later with Major and probably Princess. Macduff looked as if she was about to say something, but after second thoughts, she remained silent.

Saying that he was tired and wanted to lie down on the bed for a while, Ham disappeared into the bedroom. They heard his phone ring a couple of times and one side of muffled conversations, but he stayed in his room for the rest of the afternoon.

When he surfaced, he looked happy and refreshed. After the obligatory mug of tea, he prepared a meal for everyone. Janet and Macduff helped. Jaimie who admitted to being such a bad cook that he would burn Corn Flakes became the chief potato peeler.

After the meal, Jaimie washed the dishes, pot and pans. Macduff dried and tidied them away, claiming she knew where they went. Together in the living room, they sat and chatted about nothing particular. The discussion came round to siblings and spouses. Jaimie said that he had a baby brother who was planning to join either the Royal Marines or the RAF the following year, he hoped that he would make the right choice because he could not stand the shame of a sibling in the RAF, he laughed. Macduff said that she had a much younger sister who lived somewhere up in Scotland, but she was not sure where. They had lost touch. Janet explained that she had many brothers and sisters, but she did not know how many or where they all were. She explained that all selkies were her relatives. Ham said that he was an only child, as once his parents had him they were so shocked, they vowed never to have any more. They laughed and moved on to other subjects.

Much later, when it was dark, Ham stated that he would take the animals out for a walk. He reminded them not to open the door for anyone. He also asked Janet not to hit Jaimie on the head should anyone come a-knocking.

Macduff walked Ham to the door. As he was putting on his jacket, he told her quietly that she and Jaimie could return to their respective accommodation on his return. He said he trusted Jaimie explicitly, but he wanted her there as a safeguard. She nodded solemnly and closed the door after him.

THE JOB INTERVIEW

Ham walked along the promenade to his favourite spot near the boating pond. There were no other pedestrians about, so Ham let Major off the leash. Ham leaned on the railings and stared out over the river. Major sat beside him, and Princes sat beside Major. He had only been there a while when he heard footsteps approaching. Major growled, and Ham indicated to him with a flick of the wrist to be quiet. He turned first his head and then standing up straight, his whole body to face the two men approaching. Only two, he was expecting three.

"Colonel Maddox, have you lost a minder?" Ham asked casually.

"I'm only here for a chat Colonel Hamilton," Maddox replied. "The other time was a misunderstanding. There's no need for any weapons or strong-arm stuff. Just want a quiet chat. He can go if you want?"

"No, no need. What can I do for you, Maddox?" Ham asked casually. Ham appeared calm and ready to listen.

"It's not what you can do for me; it's what I can do for you, Hamish."

"Really? Please go on."

"You were forced to retire for mental health reasons. I'm sure that severely affected your pension. Britain can be so expensive these days. I'm sure you know that. Just look at your bill today at Morrison's. It must be crippling on a colonel's pension." Maddox looked at Hamilton, who looked back with an expression that said, 'and?'

Two things Ham learned, he or they were under surveillance, and Maddox knew of Ham's recent promotion. Somebody had talked.

When Maddox did not continue, Ham said, "And?"

"The people I work for, know how good you are and are willing to pay a lot for your services. No, no, don't dismiss it straight away. Hear me out. You and I have crossed swords many times in the past. I know how good you are. I told my people that you were the best and they are willing to pay top dollar for the best." Ham looked as if he were considering it. Encouraged Maddox continued, "With the amount of money I'm talking about, you retire to the Caribbean, or somewhere such-like. Not here in cold and wet Largs. You could afford somewhere really nice. You'd only have to work a year or two." Ham decided it was time to bust Maddox's bubble before he got too carried away.

"I like it here in Largs," Ham stated indignantly. "I choose to live here because I like it, not because I can afford it. Until recently, this was a lovely place to live. So sorry, but I must decline your offer." Maddox's face changed, and he made to move forward towards Ham. As he did so, Major growled stood up on all fours and tensed. Princess arched her back and raised the fur on her back. Ham glanced at the animals and appreciated the show of support. Ham returned his gaze to Maddox. He signalled the animals to relax with his hand and standing his ground; calmly smiled at Maddox.

"Sir! Sir!" the bodyguard yelled. "Your back. Laser!" Maddox stopped moving. He looked at Ham, who stared back with a slight smile, denoting confidence in the situation. Maddox turned full circle and looked down at the red spot fixed on his chest. All three of them followed the second red spot as it slowly but steadily walked along the ground until it disappeared behind the bodyguard. The bodyguard turned and saw that the second red dot rested on his chest. He turned and looked at his boss as in confirmation that he too had been targeted. Ham did his best not to appear puzzled as he only knew about the first sniper's red laser sighting.

Maddox turned and faced Ham. Even in the dark light Ham could see the frustration and anger in Maddox's face. Maddox had difficulty speaking for a few moments.

Finally, he blurted, "We'll meet again, and you'll wish you had accepted my offer."

"I wish I could, really I do. Just imagine all that money. But you know what it's like for us civil servants. Low pay, shit on from above, but you get the chance to serve Queen and country." Ham shrugged his shoulders apologetically. "If I had a Union Jack, I would wrap myself in it right now." Maddox knew Ham was mocking him. He turned, called to his bodyguard and stormed off into the night. Ham hated that man with a passion, and it was a safe bet that Maddox hated him in return.

Ham turned back to the railings and waited. The animals turned and stared out over the river with him. Princess made a 'phutting' sound to show her disgust.

A NEW RECRUIT

It was about twenty minutes later that Major and Princess reacted to the two figures approaching from different directions.

"I know, I know." Ham soothed the animals.

"Evening general," Ham called out just loud enough for him to hear.

"Evening, Hamilton," came the reply.

"Rob, good job," Ham called out to the SBS operative, who approached carrying a long hard-case that contained his sniper's rifle. The animals relaxed.

"Coast clear boss, except for the other sniper. I reckon he is nearby. He targeted the heavy, so I don't think he's a threat."

"That will be my man." The general proclaimed. "He'll be along soon."

"So Hamish, do you want to discuss everything here or in your flat?"

"I know you are only after my whisky, but you'll have to wait," Ham replied. "Sergeant Ingram is fully read into the operation. How about your man?"

"Oh, I think you'll find he's in up to his neck. We'll wait 'til he decides to grace us with his presence." The general walked to the railings and stared out over the river as Ham had done earlier. They waited. And they waited some more. "Very cautious chap." He turned and looked landward into the darkness. "Maybe a bit too cautious."

"He's coming now," stated Ham without emotion, not even bothering to take his eyes from the river. Major and Princess confirmed this a moment later.

A tall, dark figure carrying a similar long hardcase to Rob's emerged from the darkness. He wore a black jacket, trousers, boots and a balaclava pulled back off his head. As he drew closer, they all turned to face the stranger.

"Evening Rob. Nice night for it," came the greeting.

"Evening, John," Rob replied casually. "I thought you were with the inquisitors."

"I told you it was sanctioned, mate."

"Sergeant Peterson, late of the SBS, was recruited by Naval Intelligence, and I have recruited him to our department. He has been undercover in Maddox's company for quite a few months. He knows about the kelpies and a bit about the other cryptids, so he might as well come in full time. I think we are going to need every man we can get for this operation." Ham looked at John, at Rob and back to John. Seeing Rob's slight nod, he nodded in agreement.

"Right, now that that's settled, let's get on." The general looked around to see if there was anyone nearby. At that time of night, Ham would have been surprised if there was. The general's manner reminded Ham of the comedy TV series, 'Allo Allo,' where the characters in the French resistance would always look around exaggeratedly before speaking to check to see that the Germans were nowhere near. It was an old programme and Ham smiled a little at the memory.

"Where do you want to start?" he asked. Ham thought he was going to say, 'Listen carefully. I shall say this only once'.

"Macduff." Stated Ham. "How was she recruited?"

"You've read her file. A good officer who got into trouble. Too good to throw on the rubbish heap. I've been looking for unconventional officers to replace our losses. She seemed to fit the profile." At this point he had the candour to mention, "I served with her father in Oman. He saved my bacon more than once." Ham groaned. "You seem to have a problem with her?" The statement was a question.

"Either she or Edwards or both has been turned. Maddox is offering a lot of money. He offered me a lot tonight. Where there's money, there is temptation."

"It's not Edwards. I have him vetted regularly. I know anyone can be changed, but I'll stake my life that it's not him."

"If it's not him, it's her; please give him another check. To be sure," he added quietly.

"Why do you think she's working for the other side?" the general asked.

"Someone told Maddox that we were going to the Shetlands to see Jack Drummond. They were waiting for us. They knew where we were, even after we ditched the transponders. They knew about Janet being a selkie. Yes, they might have been following us and tracked Macduff when Janet returned, but it was just too pat. They were ready for her. Anything from the inquisitors on the two we captured?" The general shook his head. Ham continued, "Maddox knew I'd gone shopping for food today. Ok, he might have had us surveilled, but he also knew when I came out tonight; exactly when. Again that might be coincidence or good surveillance, but I don't like coincidences. I suspected that something might happen tonight, that's why I asked Rob to set up a sniper position." Ham stopped for a few moments. Maxwell could see that he was thinking and did not interrupt.

"I asked you to look into Macduff's family, especially her missing sister. Any joy?"

"Still ongoing. A bit of a wild child, by all accounts. Met a handsome young Scot and followed him north against her parent's wishes. Then she and the young man disappeared." The general cocked his head to one side. "Do you think it's Maddox's work?"

"I wouldn't put it past him. It's getting difficult to keep Macduff out of the operation. But I must do if I can't trust her." Ham spoke as if he were considering his options to himself. "Ok, we play her along for a while and take it as it comes. Can you monitor her phone and texts? I've told Rob of my fears, and now you two know. I haven't told Jaimie or Janet. A thought about the mole; why did Edwards, call himself Thompson to Macduff?"

"I told him to. I have to admit that something about Macduff didn't smell right."

"Ah, so you knew or at least suspected then." The general shrugged a non-committal gesture.

"Next, the actual operation. It's in two parts, one tomorrow night and if we find what I think we will, the second part as soon as we can arrange after that. I've talked it over with Rob. We will need all your muscle to get what we need on both nights. I asked Rob to write out the plan and prepare a list of the logistics to carry it out. I warn you; it's pretty extreme this time."

"It always is with you," the general replied.

"Firstly, can you check that Maddox is really out of the US team? I don't want to start a war with our American cousins. If he is, what about Dave Slaughter? He used to be Maddox's second in command. Did he take over? He was a good man. If he's in charge, it would be good if they could join us for the second part of the operation."

"Secondly, Do you remember Norway?" Ham asked suddenly out of the blue. The general nodded with a puzzled look on his face.

"Yes, you cheated at cards."

"I did not. My little skill allows me to know what you had. I mean, the Norwegian team we worked with on the troll business."

" Ah yes, the specialist group from the FSK, Forsvarets Spesialkommando. Go on."

"The team we worked with to move the trolls, they know about the cryptids and of course have special forces training. Could we get them for part two of the plan, the assault? I don't want our special forces near the cryptids. Already too many people know." The general nodded.

"It's an idea; I'll see what I can do. Let me have your plan and your requirements, and I'll see if I can work miracles for you. I'll get back to you. What do you want to do with Paterson here? He's all yours." Rob handed the general the pieces of paper, which he took and without reading, and stuffed into his pocket.

"Rob will take him back to his accommodation. I want him kept clear of Macduff for the moment. General, as I said, I've arranged to meet the kelpie tomorrow at dusk. We need a lot of heavy persuasion from you to 'the powers that be' to get the co-operation and equipment we need."

"It's what I do best Colonel Hamilton. It's what I do best. I'll call you." And with that, he left.

Ham nodded to Rob and John. "I'll be sending Jaimie back to you and Macduff back to her Airbnb. John, stay out of sight until we board the boat tomorrow. Rob will tell you when and what to bring. No need to watch Macduff. She can't tell Maddox anything new, and I'll point her in the wrong direction anyway. I'll keep Janet with me. I think she will be safer there. Rob, send Jaimie over after breakfast, and I'll come over to your place. I want to have a good talk with John. Goodnight lads."

Ham called the cat and dog and walked back to the apartment.

"Right, you bastard." Yelled Rob "I could have killed you in the flat. What the hell were you doing?"

"I could have killed you, you mean," John shouted back. He then grinned and continued in a softer tone, "You're getting soft in your old age. Sorry about Jaimie. I did not know it was him."

"You'll see him later, but don't apologise too much, he'll think we care. There's a whisky in the apartment. I reckon we could have one." Rob suggested. They left, and the waters of the Clyde continued to lap on the shore as if nothing had happened.

HIDE AND SECRETS

It was six in the evening when the Royal Navy patrol boat picked up Ham, Janet and the three operators from Largs pier. Ham wore his usual olive-green Barbour jacket and chinos; he did not carry anything. Janet wore a loose yellow oilskin anorak over a beige jumper and dark blue jeans. She carried a large canvas bag containing her seal skin. The operators wore casual clothes and carried large dry-sack bags containing some of their gear. More would be waiting on board the ship. Macduff wore a black jacket and slacks and an angry expression. She was staying, and she was not happy.

They stood on the pier watching the boat approach from upriver.

"Who is the third guy?" Macduff asked petulantly.

"One of their colleagues. He's just there to assist them if they have to dive and look after their boat if they have to reconnoitre."

"Rockall you say? I thought that was just a little pimple of rock sticking up in the middle of nowhere?"

"I may be wrong, but I'll put money on Maddox's base being underneath it." He paused, then continued, "Or it could be on the Irish coast. Probably Ireland. There are a lot of hidden coves along the top coast of Eire." Ham, Major and Princess stared at the small boat as it grew bigger, Macduff stared at Ham.

"That boat is too small to go all the way to Ireland, never mind Rockall," she stated. Ham nodded.

"The patrol boat is just the taxi service; it'll pick up the kelpie and take us out to HMS Bulwark. It's an Albion class amphibious transport ship. It will take us near our targets and then we will go and have a look-see either by helicopter or watercraft. I think we'll visit Rockall first and then visit northern Ireland covertly afterwards if we must. At least that's the plan."

"Why am I not going with you?" she asked although she had asked before.

"You get the best people qualified for the job; delegation. They are much better at water reconnaissance, so they get to go out and play games in the water. I'm too bloody old so; meanwhile, I will do my command and control bit onboard Bulwark. Besides, the kelpie is waiting to meet me. You will do the hard bit, you sit and wait with Major and Princess. 'A Life on the ocean waves' is not for them. If all's well we'll be back in the morning some time."

"Janet?"

"When you can swim as good as her, you can take her place," Ham responded without emotion but a hint of sarcasm. His gaze never left the navy boat.

Macduff asked, "Do you think the kelpie knows the way?" Ham shrugged.

"Knowing how to get there underwater is a darn sight different from knowing how to get there above water. A help certainly, but I think I already know the general area. The Rockall Trough, especially near Rockall itself and near the north of Ireland is the final resting place for many dead U-boats either sunk during World War Two action or scuttled after the war in Operation Deadlight."

"Operation Deadlight?"

"After the war, the allied navies agreed to get rid of all the surrendered German submarines. Each country had a designated place to scuttle them. Some made it there; a lot sank en route for various reasons or became target practice for the victor's warships. As long as the water was deep enough, it wasn't such a problem; sunk is sunk.

"When will we know?"

"Know what?"

"What they find." Ham shrugged as if it was not important.

"I'll find out when they return to the ship. I'll update you tomorrow morning when we get back."

"You go off and relax. You can stay at my place or take the beasts with you to your place. I don't want Major left alone. He's still recovering. I'll call you if I hear anything. Take Major for a walk and then chill. There is nothing that you can do but wait."

"Yes, I'll grab a bite to eat and go back to my flat and relax. If you need me…" She left the rest unsaid. "Good night sir." In the end, she slept at Ham's place as that's where the team would return, and that's where the pet food was.

"Good night Macduff. See you tomorrow" He watched her walk off. Was she the mole? Did she sell them out to Maddox? Why? He watched as she started to walk along the promenade. Major quickly fell in step beside her. Ham did not have to see Princess's habit of scampering around until she got tired and then meowing for Major to carry her to know that it would happen.

The boat arrived, and the five climbed on board.

Ham had not been strictly honest with Macduff; he had not been honest at all. The kelpie should have no trouble retracing her steps, or strokes, or whatever he or she used as a matter of propulsion. And Ham thought that he knew where Maddox's base was hiding, and it was not anywhere near Rockall or the north of Ireland. Eilean Nan Creagan in Gaelic, or Isle of Cliffs in English, sat on the Hebrides Sea Mount in the Rockall Trough, about two hundred kilometres west of Tiree, itself the most westerly of the

Inner Hebrides. If you head due west from Tiree, apart from Eilean Nan Creagan, the next stop is America.

Eilean Nan Creagan rose straight out of the mighty Atlantic. It had no beaches, no natural harbours or shelter, just straight up and down cliffs.

The British Government had considered making it a bird sanctuary but soon realised that they did not have to bother. Nature already protected the birds. The circular rock-island rose two hundred meters from the frothing sea. Crowned with rough scrubland, rocks and holding no natural water except leftover pools of rainwater. It was a pretty inhospitable place. The government had installed a light beacon on its highest point for shipping and left it to look after itself.

That might have been the end of it, except for a file Ham had come across many years previous when he was researching aquatic cryptids in the area, it stated that the Germans had constructed, or at least started to construct, a U-boat dock inside the island, entranced through an underwater tunnel. Ham had noted the file and then dismissed it as not relevant as at that time, it did not involve cryptids.

If he was right, the team would end up at that island and hopefully could safely make their way inside and more importantly, back out of it. His earlier discussion with John on the subject had not yielded anything concrete as he had never visited it or any other of Maddox's bases.

Ham was not planning to sit in the Bulwark and wait for Janet, the kelpie and the divers; he would be as close as possible and hopefully as dry as possible. He was too old to go swimming in the freezing North Atlantic.

Ham took the boat's binoculars and watched Macduff. She was on her mobile phone. He wondered to whom she was talking. He feared the worst.

GRAVEYARD OF THE DEAD IRON FISHES

Two things happened as they passed near Eilean Nan Creagan, a helicopter took off and flew directly to Tiree passing directly over Eilean Nan Creagan on the way, and HMS Bulwark gave birth to an offshore raiding craft or ORC. The raider driven by John sped across the water under the helicopter as it flew westwards. As the pair crossed the choppy water, strangely enough, it was the kelpie and Janet who complained of sea-sickness. They were comfortable in their element under the water, but bouncing along on top of the waves upset their stomachs. The kelpie looked at Ham accusingly.

As the helicopter flew over the small island, a member of the crew shot multiple infrared photographs. These would help in the planning for the next stage.

The idea was that the noisy helicopter would either distract any lookout or radar that may be on the island while the nine-metre long ORC slowly slid into the shadow of the island. John throttled back the twin Steyr M0256K43 high-speed diesel engines.

The helicopter, a Royal Navy Merlin, flew on to Tiree, while the ORC quietly circled the island in the dark. The airport manager and the police sergeant in Tiree were aroused from their beds by the unexpected arrival. 'A technical problem. No need to worry yourself.. The helicopter engineer can fix it. Thank you, no need for help'. The helicopter problem would miraculously solve itself on a signal from the SBS boys and the return of HMS Bulwark. The crew chatted with the locals and enjoyed a hot cup of tea, 'thank you no whisky, we're flying'.

The island, known to sailors colloquy as 'the Nipple', rose vertically in a circle from the depths of the Rockall Trough on top of the Hebrides Sea Mount. Waves splashed at its base, and Ham wondered where they should start looking. It was as they passed the eastern side of the island that they spotted what could be the top of the entrance to a cave. John brought the ORC close to the side of the cliffs near the site, and the SBS operators prepared their equipment ready to dive. Janet started to remove her clothes and the kelpie stripped off the clothes given to her when she boarded the patrol boat, ready to go into the water. Poor John's eye nearly bulged out of his head. Two women stripping naked in the middle of an operation, what was going on? John thought that Janet was the most beautiful woman he had ever seen. He had noticed her at Largs pier as they had waited for the patrol boat, but here she was stipping off in front of him. John was a professional, but this was getting extremely difficult. He refocused on the handling of the boat and took deep breaths.

Just as they were about to go overboard, Rob pointed into the water. A black and white shape looked back at them. An orca, a killer whale, swam around them, and under them, and beside them. Janet was petrified. Killer whales ate seals. There was no way that she was going into the water. The kelpie watched her and seemed surprised at her fear. The kelpie transformed from the naked woman who had climbed aboard the patrol boat to the kelpie on board the ORC. The kelpie had a long face of a horse, with a main of green hair. His, her or its front arms tapered to claws used to scrape the plants from the seafloor. Its hindquarters were like those of a horse except that it had webbed feet like a diver's fins. The kelpie sprang into the water. It took a few seconds for Ham to realise what had happened. When he did, he rushed to the side of the craft, expecting to see blood and gore everywhere. Instead, he saw the kelpie and the whale staring at each other. He assumed that they were communicating. Shortly afterwards several orcas surfaced around the boat. Then they left. That was that, end of the story. Gone; one minute there, the next, gone.

"They understand that we are here to rescue my brothers and sisters. We live in peace with the orcas as you call them. They will feed elsewhere. You may now enter.

Ham looked at Janet, but she sat huddled up, shivering in the corner of the boat. Ham knew it was not the cold. Ham went over and cuddled her whispering words of comfort and encouragement. It took a few minutes, but Janet recovered. She bravely continued to undress and unpacked her seal skin from her bag. John was distracted and needed a nudge from Rob to refocus on controlling the ship. As he did so, he muttered words like gorgeous, beautiful and similar sentiments. He seemed besotted. Besotted changed to amazement as Janet donned the skin and transformed in front of him. His jaw fell.

The kelpie was in the water. Next, Janet, as a seal, splashed in beside her. Rob and Jaimie dressed in their drysuits and rebreathers followed them in.

They sank beneath the waves. John and Ham waited. Ham had stressed to the divers during the briefing on board the Bulwark that this was a reconnaissance only operation. He did not want them tangling with Maddox's men that night if they could help it. He prayed that it was possible. These guys were the experts, so all he could do was sit and wait. He looked at the cliffs to see if he thought them climbable. There must be access to the World War Two German base from above if indeed the U-boat base did exist. Doubt played on his mind. If it was not there, his revived career in MIC was going to be very short-lived.

The two SBS divers followed the kelpie and the seal, as they swam towards the small cave opening as seen from the surface. The cave entrance was only a couple of meters above the surface and several meters wide. What they discovered was a huge entrance. Like an iceberg, the largest part was underwater. The water was fairly clear, but Rob could not see the bottom or the other side of the entrance. They followed the underwater creatures inside.

The tunnel ran for about ten meters then opened into a large well lit cavern. First, the divers saw the stern of a small submarine and then the harbour's side. Surfacing slowly into the shadows, they looked around in amazement. Lights hung from the ceiling; chiselled out of the walls were several rooms, large empty metal cages sat on the paved U-shaped harbour. Rob recognised the submarine; it was the last type he expected to see there, a North Korean Sang-O-class submarine. At thirty-four meters in length it weighed in at two hundred and seventy-five tons surfaced, three hundred and seventy tons of submerged and berthed on the coast of Scotland, it was a long way from home. It was a diesel-electric coastal ship, how on earth did it get there? Its range was only two thousand eight hundred kilometres. It was very strange, but at least they knew who was paying Maddox for the kelpies; North Korea.

Rob nodded to Jaimie, who took several photos. As Ham had said, this was a reconnaissance mission, so they swam around the harbour rising in the shadows to get different views of the establishment. Seeing small cranes on the harbourside with cables hanging in the water they dived under to see where the cables led. Large metal cages sat on the bottom. Each cage contained two or three kelpies. The kelpie and Janet did not want to leave, they wanted to free the captives, but Rob and Jaimie pulled them away. Indicating that they came to look only, Rob pointed to the tunnel. Rob knew it was time to leave, and he did not want to push it. When they still seemed reluctant, he signalled again that it was time to leave. They went reluctantly. The kelpie and the selkie swam towards the tunnel.

Rob and Jaimie ascended into the shadows for one last look around before they too would leave. He cursed under his breath. Directly above them, a Korean sailor attracted by the movement in the shadows was bent over and peering over the harbour's edge. Rob and Jaimie lunged out of the water and firmly grabbed the startled sailor. He did not have time to yell out before they dragged him into the water. There was a bit of a splash, but there was no choice. They took him deep into the watery shadows of the tunnel.

To begin with, he struggled, but by the time they emerged from the other side of the tunnel, he was a lifeless form.

The kelpie and the seal led the way out and back to the boat, to a very relieved Ham. He knew from his second sight that no human in the team was going to die that night, but he was not sure that his gift worked on other species. Everyone clambered aboard. John held the Korean sailor against the side of the boat, with an expression that asked, 'What do you want me to do with this?'.

Ham thought for a moment then talked to the kelpie. She nodded, a curious human gesture Ham thought afterwards.

The kelpie dived over the side and disappeared. She returned after a while with one of the earlier orcas. The orca took the Korean sailor in his mouth and headed off towards the cave, where it would wave the body around, showing the other sailors that the man had been prey to the notorious killer whale. What happened to the sailor after that, Ham did not care.

The kelpie changed her form to a human again, and they helped her on board.

After the Bulwark had circled the Rockall a few times, sent helicopters here, there and everywhere in the general direction, it had sailed towards Eire. Still, in international waters, the helicopters had practised their equivalent of an aircraft's circuits and bumps, repeatedly landing and taking off. Returning to HMNB Clyde, still, in the dark, the HMS Bulwark picked up an ORC and a helicopter that the engineer had miraculously fixed.

Ham and his team debriefed on HMS Bulwark. Pleased with their actions that night, Ham told them the story he wanted them to tell Macduff if asked. He wanted to wait and see what the general could find out before he acted, but he knew he might not have a choice. It was a pity as he had started to like her. She would have made a solid team member, possibly a team leader in time.

A naval patrol boat met the ship and took the group from the ship near to the Isle of Cumbrae, where the kelpie went overboard after Ham had arranged where to meet again. It was impressed on the crew that the naked woman diving overboard was never to be mentioned again; ever. If some daft female skinny-dipper wanted to swim back to her island in the ice-cold water, it was nothing to do with them.

The four were dropped off at Largs pier and retired to Ham's flat for breakfast. With a mug of tea in his hand, Ham said he was too tired to cook, so they all retired to the Green Shutters. Ham paid. It truly was amazing how much the SBS operators could eat.

PLANNING, LOGISTICS AND INTRIGUE

After breakfast, Ham sent the three operators back to their temporary home. To Macduff he gave a choice, crash out on Ham's bed with Janet or go to her Airbnb. If she went to the Airbnb, he could talk more freely on the phone, but if she stayed, he could keep an eye on her. It was six and half-a-dozen. It was her choice.

He did not want Janet staying with Macduff, in case Macduff was the traitor and Janet suddenly disappeared. Janet did not seem to mind, so after a shower; she climbed under the duvet. Macduff or not, she was tired.

Ham knew he was on the sofa-bed. It was not how he had planned his retirement.

Ham grabbed Major and Princess and set off along the promenade. Reaching his favourite viewing spot, near the boating pond, he tapped in the general's direct number using his encrypted ministry issued mobile phone. He told the general what they had done and what they had seen. He asked for instructions on how to proceed. The general updated him on the search for the informer and about the general's discussions with his counterparts in America and Norway. They had agreed on a joint operation, with Ham taking the lead. It would take a couple of days for the Americans and the Norwegians to arrive in Scotland.

They discussed the equipment and services required for Ham's plan. Ham was worried that Edwards, the general's assistant, would be involved in the preparations. The general advised Ham that Edwards was busy elsewhere and that if he needed something urgent and the general was not available, to dial a number and talk to Ms Lucinda Miller. She had been briefed and was pretty good at sorting things out. Most importantly, she was discrete.

Ham asked that the general focus on finding the traitor as working with Macduff not knowing if she was the one, was getting bothersome. The general was at his most genial and said not to worry he had people on the job and expected results soon. Ham thanked him. The general said he would come back to Ham with results of the investigation soonest and cut the line.

Ham still worried though. He walked back to the flat, showered and crawled into a hastily made sofa bed. Still worried, but tired, he fell into a deep sleep.

He was woken mid-afternoon, by Macduff and a mug of tea. She wore only her bra and panties. Ham's sleepy eyebrows raised in surprise.

"Captain, you seem rather undressed to be serving tea."

"You've seen me in less." She looked at the expression on his face. "Sorry sir, I did not want to wake Janet, so I just slid out of bed."

"Well, go and slide into some clothes. You'll catch your death of cold." She skipped out of the room. Ham frowned. It was a bit bloody obvious. Was she the mole? Was she trying to distract him? Was she just naive?

Ham drank his tea and relaxed his mind; short of confronting her outright, there was nothing he could do at the moment. No, he would let the general and his investigators do their thing. He had to keep his emotions in check until he found out if she was involved with Maddox's team.

What if Maddox had kidnapped Macduff's sister and was holding her to extract information from Macduff? Would that make any difference? If she was working for the other side, she was putting every team member in peril. If she was guilty, Ham knew what he should do with her, or rather what he would recommend to the general, but Ham was human, and he had grown to like the young woman. He thought she had what it takes to be in the department, but only, only if she was clean. He also believed that she had the second sight, only that it was still deep inside her. Damn that Maddox.

Ham sent Macduff off to the shops to buy some food for that night. When she was gone, he telephoned the SBS operators, who by the sound of them had been fast asleep and stood them down for the next twenty-four hours. He hadn't wanted to call them in front of Macduff as she might inform Maddox that he was safe for the next twenty-four hours at least.

Next, he called Lieutenant Commander Fischer. Fischer answered in his annoying high and mighty manner until Ham introduced himself. Ham asked if Fischer had planted the WW2 German Seehund midget submarine in the Tan and informed Professor Sandberg. Fischer reported that he had.

Ham asked in passing if Fischer had monitored any unusual readings or sounds while testing the equipment next to the Isle of Cumbrae. Happy to talk about his baby project, Fischer explained that he had recorded some distant sounds that he could not identify properly. Ham politely enquired further. The lieutenant commander seemed to get a bit flustered.

"Well, you see sir, it's just that my sound operator says its computerised sound profile is like a North Korean Sang-O-class submarine. My equipment is not that bloody good." He brayed a laugh until he realised that Ham was not joining in. "You see, it can't be; they are only suitable for local work, around the Korean Peninsula. North Korea is on the other side of the world," he added lamely. Ham bit his tongue and decided not to tell him that he knew that. He just made noises of surprise, thanked the lieutenant and closed the call. Just like the American radar equipment on

Hawaii before the Japanese attack on Pearl Harbour; the equipment worked, but the humans ignored the information they got.

Ham decided to tell the general about Fischer's equipment's success in hearing the North Korean submarine and leave it up to him to decide how to tell him without compromising their operation.

A TRAITOR EXPOSED

The day had been quiet but strenuous for Ham maintaining a semblance of normality in the flat. Ham, Janet and Macduff took turns cooking, washing up and drying. Everyone decided that Janet was by far the better cook. The conversation was light and mainly irrelevant. Ham felt restricted. He did not want to discuss operational matters in front of Macduff, and it was with a deeply felt appreciation that he was called and summoned to the promenade that evening. The general said he was to bring Macduff, so Ham guessed that the general had found out sufficient evidence of what was going on. The revelation made Ham sad, but he tried not to show it.

Just before the appointed hour, Ham gathered Macduff and the beasts and headed off down the promenade. They found the general alone stood halfway between the RLNI slipway and the boating pond, leaning as Ham was wont to do, on the railings. He turned as they approached. He greeted them cheerfully and shook Ham's hand.

"Good job with the 'reccy' on the island. You handled the Korean sailor well." Being the first time Macduff had heard of anything to do with Korean sailors, she viewed Ham with suspicion. As she suspected, he was keeping stuff from her.

"Sir, you called us here," Ham stated, getting to the point.

"Yes, yes. Firstly, we've found out who the traitor was in our midst. That bloody viper at our breast. Edwards. You know him as Thompson," he said, looking at Macduff.

"The investigators found his secret bank account and the money he received from Maddox." Macduff mind juggled with thoughts.

"What will happen to him?" asked Ham matter of factly. He was relieved it was not Macduff but did not show it.

"Who else did you suspect general?" Macduff asked calmly. Maybe a little bit too calmly.

"Why you, of course, dear." The general replied cheerily. "We had to check you out of course. You being the new gal on the block so to speak."

"What's the story on Macduff's sister?" Ham knew that he had just stepped into a minefield and that it was going to be messy. But he felt he had to ask. Edwards might be the traitor, but it did not mean that he was the only one.

Macduff was not out of the woods yet. Ham saw Macduff staring at him incredulously. He had just stepped on the first mine, boom!

"Oh, we found her and her Welsh husband on a sheep farm in Snowdonia, living the rustic life. Some people don't seem able to tell the difference between the Welsh and the Scottish. By all accounts, they are happy and expecting their first." Macduff was still staring angrily at Ham. Ham stared her down; he had to ask. He was damned if he was going to be bullied by a subordinate.

"What will happen to Edwards?" Ham asked.

"Nothing now. Edwards had a little fatal road traffic accident this morning. Tragic coincidence." Ham felt another boom from the minefield. Both Ham and Macduff looked at the general with disbelief. The general smiled innocently. The general, oblivious of the mess Ham was in with Macduff, might have got away with it, but he added, "Did you expect him to go to prison quietly?" Ham accepted judgement and action; it was a road traffic accident, and he was sure nobody could prove otherwise. He had seen the general in action before. He was ruthless. Macduff, on the other hand, had other thoughts.

"What if it had been me? Would I have had a little fatal road traffic accident?" She was visibly upset.

"Ham, you speak to her later and explain our situation better. Macduff, we are a close-knit group that relies on each other for survival. He took two million dollars and didn't give a damn what happened to you all." And as far as the general was concerned, that was that.

"To get back to business. Ham fill in Macduff later. I'll fill you in the details and gaps later; the nitty-gritty so to speak. You'll all be picked up by a patrol boat tomorrow midday. It'll take you to HMNB Clyde. There you will meet the Norwegians, three of them; you have worked with Magnus." It was a statement, but Ham nodded. You'll all fly to Tiree airport. Sergeant Ingram and Corporal Nicholls, our SBS heroes, will stay on board. The Americans will be off Tiree tomorrow waiting for them. I'll send you the details later. Stealth is the order of the day, so your two boys will need to be helicoptered out to the submarine early so that it can get into a position closer to the island. They've done the helicopter to submarine fast-roping bit many times before, so it should not be a problem. They'll meet Cmdr. Dave Slaughter and his boys from the US Navy SEALs on board. We'll be using their equipment this trip, ours is either being used elsewhere or is in the repair shop. Makes the Americans feel useful what?"

"The helicopter from the navy base will have an offshore raiding craft underslung. Sergeant Paterson and the Norwegians will be dropped off offshore with the craft before you get to Tiree. There is a sheltered bay on the east of the island near the Tiree ferry terminal, but I'll leave that stuff up to you. Hamish you and Captain Macduff will be landed at the airport where you will drink tea and eat scones while you wait until it is time to kickoff. The photos taken by the helicopter flyover will be waiting for you at Faslane[33]. I'll send you the details of everything

---

[33] HMNB Clyde

I have tonight and leave you to brief your team individually." He turned to face Macduff. "I am so glad it wasn't you, my dear. Do give my best to your father when you see him." Macduff, totally engrossed in the plan that she knew nothing about, suddenly returned to the realisation that if they thought that she had been the traitor, she might have been in a nasty accident. Strangely, she did not blame the general; instead, she glared at Ham. Boom went another landmine.

The general wished them luck and wandered off into the darkness with a cheery grin on his face. They saw his bodyguard skirt the shadows and follow him. 'Bastard', thought Ham, 'Dropped me right in it'.

For the rest of the evening, the atmosphere was on the chilly side. Ham waited for the courier with the latest intelligence and details. When Macduff realised that Janet was involved in the operation on the island and had not told her, the temperature in the flat got damn right freezing.

When the courier did arrive, Ham read through the papers. He did this with a mug of tea made by Janet as Macduff was giving him the cold shoulder. Ham had had enough. When he finished reading the documents, he stood up and walked to the window.

"Read that lot, please. Both of you." He called over his shoulder. He then called Rob and told him to come over. He also said that he would expect them all over for breakfast. He turned to see Janet and Macduff devouring the paperwork. Now he would see how professional

Macduff was. This time was when he would decide if she had a future in the team.

"Right, plan for tonight, Macduff you go back to your flat, be here at eight. Janet, sorry, but, I need a good night's sleep, and I want to see what my bed feels like," she raised an eyebrow, "you can go with Macduff, or you're on the sofa tonight. You and you," pointing at the animals, "are in your beds tonight. Got it." Major raised an eyebrow, and the kitten yawned disinterestedly.

THE PRELUDE TO AN OPERATION

Ham woke refreshed, to find the dog in the cat's tiny bed and the cat in the huge dog's bed, typical. Janet was fast asleep on the couch. He prepared the coffee machine and went for the three S's, shit, shower and shave. As he walked back to his room, he passed Janet. She walked naked, wiping the sleep from her eyes. With her arms raised to her face, her ample bosoms thrust firmly forward. She had no idea of the effect her figure had on the average male, and although Ham was old, he was average.

After dressing Ham put away Janet's bedding and folded away the sofa bed. He made two coffees and entered the lounge. One mug went on the coffee table, the other he took to the bay window, where he watched the ferry sailing back and forth to the island, and the cars queuing to get on the ferry. He watched the dog walkers and the keep-fit fanatic passing beneath his gaze. Everything was so normal. He knew that within hours he and his team would be embarking on a perilous mission. Through his second sight, he knew they would all survive, at least the humans, but he could not see if any would be injured.

Some people might say, so what if a foreign power kidnapped a few underwater creatures, they are nothing better than fish, but to Ham, they were just as human as he was. Also, the kelpies were replenishing their stock from the human population with their simple; you take one of ours; we take one of your's philosophy. Ham had no idea what the North Koreans wanted to do with the kelpies. Either they did not know how peace-loving and pacifist the kelpies were, or they thought they could brainwash them into warriors. They were like underwater cows. Could someone train a docile cow to fight? He thought about it. Probably, the Spanish did. The shape-shifting kelpies could be a dangerous force if the North Koreans could militarise them.

Ham heard Janet come in and pick up her coffee. "I don't know what the fuss was about; the sofa-bed is quite comfortable. I could just as easily stayed in your bed." Ham turned a look of shock on his face. "What?" she asked coyly. "You think I am too old for you." She giggled. "I am only just over two hundred years old." Ham was speechless.

He eventually spluttered a reply, "Jack… Jack…"

"Yes, I know you were Jack's best friend. You know the last thing Jack said to me upstairs in our cottage? Go with Hamish and look after him. He's a good man, and he will treat you well."

"I don't think Jack meant…"

"I think I know what Jack meant; I was married to him for over thirty years. You forget Hamish Hamilton that I am a selkie, not a human. We think differently." Ham looked at the young woman in front of him and thought, 'I don't need this kind of crap today of all days'. Luckily the main door security buzzer sounded, Rob, Jaimie and John had arrived. Macduff arrived a few moments later. He was glad to see that she appeared to be in a good mood.

They went to the Green Shutters for breakfast, where they talked trivial matters ignoring the elephant in the room.

They would discuss the operation when they returned to the flat.

After breakfast, Ham sent Macduff over to the island to find the kelpie, which should be waiting in horse form where it was before. Macduff did so and arranged a meeting for a couple of hours later. Job done, Macduff returned to the team.

By midday, they were ready. All other matters and grievances pushed elsewhere; they had about enough things on their plate as it was.

The patrol boat arrived at the pier, and they sailed up the Clyde to the naval base, with a slight detour to pick up the kelpie in female form. He nakedness caused a few raised eyebrows among the crew, but a quiet word in their ear brought them back on track. Janet had brought clothes for the girl. The humans sat or stood in their thoughts as the boat plied through the calm waters. The selkie sat quietly, apparently without a care in the world, the kitten slept on her lap, while the dog enjoyed the breeze. The journey was short, and a young officer escorted them to the helipad, where a twin-engine heavy-lift Boeing chinook helicopter from Seven Squadron Joint Special Forces Aviation Wing, awaited them. The SBS men immediately checked the equipment they had requested.

Ham saw Magnus and the two members of his team dressed in combats and loaded down with all their equipment escorted by the Master coming towards them. Major Magnus Munsen shook Ham's hand and introduced his team; Løtnant[34] Karoline Hauger and Sersjantmajor[35]

---

[34] Norwegian lieutenant

Mathias Berland. Ham stared for a moment at the løtnant. Ham was not surprised to see a female special forces operator in their team as the Norwegians embraced sexual equality. Karoline was there because she was good, not because of her sex.

They walked over to the helicopter and the team introduced to the SBS operators. John and Rob greeted them in Norwegian explaining that they had trained many times in Norway with 42 Commando. The SBS operators helped the FSK team stow away their equipment, some in the helicopter and some they tied down in the ORC parked nearby on a trolley. Jaimie was more than pleased to help Karoline with her equipment. The tall thin long-blonde-haired beauty smiled at him in return. Mathias, a well built

---

[35] Norwegian sergeant major

dark-haired, dark-eyed, dark-skinned giant, from northern Norway, smiled; he had seen this many times with foreign operators. Thanking the Master for his help, the teams boarded the Chinook. Ham confirmed the next stage of the operation with the captain, and it lifted off to hover over the ORC where the aircrew and ground grew underslung the craft. Once it was safely secured, they set off for Tiree. Onboard Ham briefed Magnus on the basics of the plan. He said he would explain further when they were at their destination; it was far too noisy in the helicopter.

Everyone was used to the helicopter flying, but it was only Princess who slept. She had found Karoline's lap as suitable for the purpose. Karoline thought this most amusing. She had never seen a cat, never mind a kitten taken on a mission.

Major dressed in his harness, lay at Ham's feet, his eyes continually roving around the gathering. Ham suddenly gasped when hit by a foul smell. Major looked accusingly at Ham and moved away to Macduff. Rob and Jaimie started to look accusingly at Ham.

"It's the bloody dog!" said Ham forcibly pointing at Major who did his best to look innocent. Macduff tutted and then laughed. Her laugh was infectious and broke the tense atmosphere. They all laughed at the silliness of it all. That is until Major let rip again, causing Macduff to gag. Janet moved away from the dog. Major looked offended.

"Major you arsehole!" Macduff blurted involuntarily.

"Pardon me?" questioned Major Magnus Munsen. Major, the dog, had not been introduced to major the major. That set them off again. Rob explained to the major.

They sat in silence for the rest of the trip. Ham tried not to stare at the løtnant, but he found it difficult. It was not her beauty that attracted his gaze. He had seen her short future. He knew she was going to die soon, and it would be a violent death. He also knew that he could do nothing about it. You cannot change your future.

Ham suddenly remember that Magnus was also a boundary walker. Why had he allowed løtnant Karoline Hauger to come on the mission? He looked over at the major and found the major looking back at him. Magnus shook his head slowly. Magnus's Second Sight had told him the same future for the Norwegian officer. Ham got the message; they would talk later.

BOAT AWAY

The Chinook came to a halt, John, the kelpie and the Norwegians descended through a hatch and fast roped down to the boat. The kelpie followed instructions and did so as if she did it all the time. The helicopter lowered, and the boat with the operators settled onto the water. The ORC engines started, and they cast off. The aircrew raised the thick rope as the helicopter lifted away.

Flying to Tiree airport, the helicopter landed and deposited Ham, Janet, Macduff and the beasts. Taking off straight away, the Chinook flew off to the west for the rendezvous with the American submarine.

The helicopter flew until it arrived at the agreed co-ordinates, there the helicopter met with a surfacing Benjamin Franklin-class former ballistic missile nuclear submarine: the USS Kamehameha. The SBS operators were not concerned with missiles; their interest lay in the two large DDSs, Dry Deck Systems, built on the deck behind the conning tower over where the missile silos had once been. The US Navy reclassified the submarine as an attack submarine after the addition of the two dry decks or hangers. The SBS operators fast-roped down to the deck. They had done so many times to similarly built British submarines. On the deck, a young officer took them down inside the vessel.

Job done, the chinook returned to Tiree airport. The submarine sank into the waves and headed off towards its lay-up point near Eilean Nan Creagan. Inside, after being introduced to the captain, the SBS men were introduced to Cmdr. Dave Slaughter, who later, in turn, introduced them to his specialist SEAL team, Lt. Joe Pottkamp, a tall blond giant and CPOs, chief petty officers Sam Wainwright, a short, slim brown-haired wiry man with a glint of fun in his eyes and David Apps, an elderly, by special forces standards being at least thirty-five, mass of moving muscle with a face that had met many a punch in its time. David Apps' voice matched his look; it was a growl.

"So they haven't caught you yet," he growled.

"Still hitting the other guy's fist with your face." Came the reply. Apps and Ingram shook hands and slapped each other on the shoulder. They had shared missions before. A commonality found, the two teams sat and discussed the mission in a calm, professional manner mixed with the odd comical reference to each other's service.

John drove the ORC into the small harbour in front of the Scarnish Hotel near the Tiree Ferry Terminal. The bay was more secluded, not that Tiree was busy. Mathias volunteered to stay with the boat while the others walked the short distance up to the hotel. There they ordered a round of beers and a meal. The kelpie took a sip of a beer and decided that water was the better choice. When John introduced her to carbonated or bubbly water, she giggled and laughed at the experience, lightening the atmosphere of the team. They chatted about inconsequential things and appeared very relaxed. After a while, John went down and relieved Mathias at the boat so that he too could eat, drink and relax with the rest.

Ham, Janet and Macduff went to the airport terminal where they found coffee, tea and snacks available with an honesty box. They waited for the helicopter to return. When it did, Ham checked with the aircrew that all was in order. Satisfied that all was going to plan, Ham contacted John who told him that they were at the hotel. The four-man aircrew and two Force Protection airmen from the RAF Regiment said they would stay with their helicopter and chill. Ham summoned a taxi which drove Ham, the ladies and the beasts to the hotel, where they too enjoyed a beer, or water and a light late lunch. An agreement was arranged with the taxi driver to take them back to the airport later.

Ham explained to the kelpie her role in the upcoming operation. He also found time to talk to Magnus away from the others.

Returning to the airport, Ham and Macduff found time alone to discuss the matter of the traitor investigation. She was calmer and able to understand the need for secrecy. When she said, 'I don't know if I can be that ruthless.', Ham replied, 'you will. In time you will. When it's a matter of protecting your team, you will'. The matter closed, Janet joined them, and they chatted generally.

BOAT UP, BOAT DOWN

Being given a choice to remain at the airport, or go with the helicopter, Ham, Janet and Macduff chose to fly, along with the beasts which did not have the choice. They took off and headed for the water just outside the small bay where the ORC had docked. The ORC, containing John and the Norwegians was waiting for them. The helicopter hovered over the craft, and the cables lowered. Once they hooked the boat up, the aircrew winched the passengers back up into the chinook. They could not have parked the ORC at the airport because they did not have a trolley to support it. The last thing Ham wanted was a damaged ORC. He could not take that chance.

The chinook, complete with ORC ascended and flew west towards Eilean Nan Creagan. It was only flying halfway. The OCR was going in under its own power, but the helicopter lift had reduced the time and distance it had to travel on the open sea. The weather was always going to be an unknown factor. The forecast was good, but nature does not always play by the rules, especially on the west coast of Scotland.

Leaving the ORC and its crew on relatively calm water to make its way to Eilean Nan Creagan, the helicopter returned to Tiree airport. Another chinook waited for them. Ham's chinook parked next to its twin. As it came to a stop, the RAF ground crew that came with the second chinook ran a hose from a fuel bladder stored in the hold to

Ham's aircraft. They would need a full tank to get to the island and back safely.

Ham, Macduff, Janet and the beasts wandered around and kept themselves out of the way. They would be the last element to hit the island and had time to kill.

"Are all your plans this complicated?" Macduff asked.

"No, this is a simple one," he replied and walked on. "A straight forward pincer with a backup. You should have seen the one to move Bigfoot up to the Canadian reservation. Now that was complicated," he muttered.

They had time to kill, so Ham told them of some of the missions, he and other members of the department had carried out over the years. He was not bragging; this was part of Macduff's training. If Janet decided to stay with the team, it would be part of her training as well. The cryptids he mentioned were varied, and the locations were as near and far as the globe was round; the mountains high, and the oceans deep. Ham had worked in Ireland, Nepal, America, Australia and South America, to name a few. The list went on. It was a prescription to ruin any marriage, days, weeks sometimes months away from home. Ham looked at Macduff.

"You've got to have a very understanding boyfriend or husband," he warned her.

"Yes, like you said before, plenty of sex and travel."

"I didn't say anything about sex!" he exclaimed; she laughed; Janet laughed; he groaned.

"Focus captain. You can think about your sex life after the mission." Ham moaned.

"Yes, boss." She smirked at Janet, who grinned back at her.

BABY SUB

In the submarine, the SEALs and SBS operators dressed and prepared their equipment. Checking their watches one last time, Cmdr. Dave Slaughter led the five operators up through the hatch into one of the drydocks built on the USS Kamehameha. The SBS operators used a similar system on the UK's Royal Navy Astute class submarines such as HMS Artful, using their version of the DDS, the SFPB, the Special Forces Payload Bay, which some wag had nicknamed 'the caravan of death'. They climbed into the Mark 8 Mod 1 SDV, or Seal Delivery Vehicle, an open-to-the-water six-person submersible, with the help of the support divers. The Royal Navy, not having SEALS, called their SDVs, Swimmer Delivery Vehicles. But they were the same. It was just under seven meters in length and just under two meters in width. With a full team of six, it could travel about sixteen kilometres, which should be more than enough for this mission. Chief Petty Officer David, not Dave but David please, Apps was the pilot with Lt. Joe Pottkamp as the co-pilot. The passengers sat facing backwards. Behind Apps sat the commander and Rob sat beside him. CPO Sam Wainwright and Jaimie sat to the rear of them. With everything checked and secured, the hanger flooded and the large circular door opened. The support divers assisted the rolling out of the SDV. The operators supplemented their rebreathers using compressed air tanks on the SDV.

The submersible left the hangar and guided by the Doppler Inertial Navigation System, headed towards Eilean Nan

Creagan at a speed of four knots, about seven and a half kilometres per hour. Bubbles bled to the surface initially, but as they approached the target, they would switch to their rebreathers. Rebreathers, circulate and scrub the carbon-dioxide and add a little oxygen, allowing the divers to rebreathe the same air again. The motor was electric, and when they all used the rebreather systems, no tell-tale bubbles would rise to the surface.

As they slowly made their way underwater, the ORC sped over the waves to the same destination. John drove the craft skillfully navigating the large waves and skimming over the small waves. The kelpie fought back her seasickness; life above the ocean waves was not to her liking. The Norwegians checked their equipment and the surroundings. All was secure, and all was clear.

Ham, Macduff and Janet, talked, walked and waited. They knew that the other two teams were converging on the island and there was nothing they could do in Tiree but wait for their turn.

THE FIRST ARRIVALS

They left the SDV just inside the shelter of the tunnel on the floor. Having exited the craft, they swam through the tunnel and into the large cavern. David and Rob swam under the North Korean Submarine and after setting the timers attached limpet mines to the underside of the hull. Whatever happened in the next couple of hours, the submarine was not going back to North Korea.

Joe Slaughter and Sam Wainwright swam to the cages. Even though they knew from the briefing what to expect, they were still startled by the creatures that greeted them. Indicating for the kelpies to move away from the door to the cage, Joe and Sam attached small charges to the locks. The timid kelpies were content to stay away from the strange black men-like creatures and their activities. The small explosive was a thermite charge which melted rather than exploded the lock. It was quick and would only be seen from above if someone was looking directly at that spot in the water. With the doors open, Joe and Sam ushered the kelpies out and guided them towards the tunnel and freedom. There were four cages, and the men worked from one to the next. When they had finished, they rejoined their commander at the tunnel entrance.

Rob guided Joe Slaughter to various points that he had visited with Jaimie on the previous visit. They then returned to the rendezvous point and waited for the team to assemble. Limpets attached, cages vacated, the team gathered. Maintaining radio silence, Slaughter indicated where he wanted the team to go. Much of it had already been agreed beforehand after the briefing from Rob and Jaimie. Slaughter was making final adjustments to the plan; after sending a burst signal to Ham, signalled the others to wait. Typical military rush and wait, rush and wait. He checked and rechecked his watch.

While the underwater team was doing this, John and the Norwegians approached the sheer cliffs of the island's side.

The kelpie stripped off her borrowed clothes and dived into the water where she disappeared into the dark green waters.

They secured the ORC to the base of the cliff, and Løtnant Karoline Hauger started to climb up the vertical wall trailing a rope behind her. Although she had AN/PVS-14 night vision technology attached to her helmet, she preferred to work without, using touch and feel. Serjantmajor Matthias Berland hitched himself to the rope and followed her. The major went next; John followed suit. The climb was long and straight up, but it was not taxing as there were plenty of hand and footholds. Karoline, Mathias and the major were expert climbers, John had the training but was not an expert. Even he found the going relatively easy. Reaching the top, they tied off the rope. They would probably need it to get back to the ORC.

Mathias scouted the area on top of the cliff using night vision optics and found no sign of life. He returned, and they agreed to spread out and search further. They used their helmet-mounted night vision system to aid in their search. John wore the UK's HMNVS or Head Mounted Night Vision System.

After half an hour of cautious investigation, they found the camouflaged entrance and returned to the rendezvous point on top of the cliffs. Major Munsen sent the short burst signal that they too were ready to enter the complex. They had also received Slaughter's message that the seal team was ready.

Ham and Macduff were already on the chinook. Major would travel with them; after all, he was a military dog. Ham tried unsuccessfully to get Janet to remain behind on Tiree with Princess. He had brought Janet as a safeguard in case the plan needed adjusting, and her swimming skills were required. Princess made it clear that she was not staying behind. Ham gave Janet a spare Browning nine-millimetre High power that he carried. He showed her how to work the safety and aim and fire. She explained that Jack had already shown her many times how to handle a weapon. As soon as the two messages were received Ham signalled the chinook crew that they were good to go. The helicopter rose and headed off towards Eilean Nan Creagan; the flight would take about forty minutes. They flew low over the waves. The aircrew manning the two M134 miniguns on the side of the aircraft and Force Protection airmen operating the M60 machine gun at the rear checked their weapons, firing test shots into the water. The second RAF Regiment airman checked his rifle and sat calmly waiting for the landing.

The aircrew advised Ham that they were getting close, about ten kilometres out. He signalled the two teams.

The SEALS with their SBS counterparts made their way to their agreed positions and stealthily exited the water, leaving their bulky rebreathers behind. An armed civilian turned a corner of a building in the cavern, spotted Slaughter and was shot by Slaughter's suppressed weapon before he could raise the alarm. The teams moved around the underground harbour moving where possible from shadow to shadow. Jaimie moved into a position where he could cover the submarine's conning tower. The other cautiously checked around buildings. With hand signals, they all moved stealthily into position. They waited.

Meanwhile, The FSK operatives and John Paterson moved to and entered the concealed entrance and descended the steps. There was a metal door, but it was unlocked and unarmed, they were not expecting visitors. The team carried on with stealth, ready for exposure at any time.

The chinook flew closer. Ham wondered if he really should have insisted that Janet stayed behind. Princess lay curled in his Barbour pocket. He hoped that was not a mistake either. The Guardian would be most pissed if something happened to the princess.

Ham had said that he wanted to take prisoners wherever possible, but the general had insisted that that was not to happen. The cryptids must be protected, and any prisoners would find themselves hidden away for the rest of their lives in mental hospitals or remote prisons in solitary confinement. The general, a practical man, said that was too expensive. When this mission was over, no witnesses were to be left. Ham was not a violent man by nature, but he also understood the practical necessity. This operation never happened; it was not a Black Op; it was darker.

The chinook climbed as it neared the island; the noise increased as the helicopter landed. The RAF Regiment airman ran out and knelt ready to protect the aircraft; the other operated the onboard machine gun.

Armed civilians and North Korean sailors hearing the helicopter rushed out of buildings and rooms into a hail of bullets coming at them from all angles. A firefight ensued. Different weapons fired in a cacophony of differing sounds. The operator's suppressed weapons phutted and spluttered death but Maddox's men and the few North Korean sailors fired a variety of deafening firearms. Fragmentation grenades exploded.

An officer appeared on top of the conning tower with a pistol in his hand, Jaimie shot, and blood spurted from the man's head. He disappeared. Another head peaked over the side to meet a similar fate. Jaimie could hear klaxons sounding within the submarine. Jaimie ran from his position and boarded the submarine. He lobbed a grenade up onto the conning tower. When it exploded, he quickly climbed up and looked in. He saw several bodies and weapons lying in a bloody mess. He shot them again to make sure that they were dead and dropped another grenade down into the hatch. He heard screams before the grenade exploded.

Closing the hatch, he set off a thermite grenade which fused the hatch shut as it melted through the metal. He proceeded to do the same at every hatch he could find on the ship's deck.

Slaughter, Wainright, Apps and Ingram cleared buildings together, opening doors, tossing in 'flash-bangs', concussion grenades that exploded with a bright light, disorientating those inside the room, the operators followed in a practised sequence covering the sides, front and the corridor. There were no hostages to worry about so anybody in those rooms was a target. It was easier than the training in the 'Killing House', but each door could be their last. There could be booby traps or equally experienced professionals on the other side. They worked mechanically.

John and the FSK operators dealt similarly with anyone coming up the stairs or in the rooms leading off the staircase. John had not worked with the FSK before but could see that they were a well-trained team. He controlled the corridor as they took the rooms.

Ham ran with Macduff and Janet to the entrance now marked with red smoke left by the FSK team. Major beat them to it. Knowing that the team had cleared the stairwell, they proceeded quickly but cautiously down. Major proceeded them.

Major flew at a man coming the other way. The impact of a dog pouncing on out of nowhere seemed to cause him confusion. Ham put him out of his confusion with two shots. They moved on.

The fire-fight continued for ten more minutes while the enemy combatants were discovered and killed. No surrender or quarter was asked or given.

Using his throat mike, Ham asked if anyone had seen Maddox. Nobody had. He gave the order for charges laid around the cavern and entrance to cause their destruction. The SEAL team had already laid charges in the tunnel while they had waited which would ensure its collapse after they left.

Ham, Slaughter and Munsen met and agreed that it was time to go, the kelpies were released and were being guided home by the kelpie the FSK team brought to the island, the submarine mined, and the secret harbour was primed ready to be destroyed.

It still bothered Ham that they did not find Maddox. Maybe he was off the island and up to no good elsewhere. It was time to go.

The SEAL-SBS team collected and adjusted their equipment, re-entered the water and headed for the SDV in the tunnel. John, the FSK team, accompanied by Janet and Major, ran up the stairway back to the helicopter. Macduff waited for Ham as he looked around one last time. This place was historical. If the Germans had managed to get it operational, the U-boats using it would have caused chaos to allied shipping. In less than half an hour, it would disappear into history, just like the U-boats that littered the floor of the Rockall Trough outside.

Princess suddenly meowed and dug her claws sharply into Ham's stomach, causing him to suddenly jack-knife in pain. A bullet winged passed where his head had been. Still bent over, he looked over and glimpsed the figure of Maddox as he dived into the water at the opposite end of the harbour from the tunnel entrance. Macduff reacted first, firing at the fleeing figure, Ham fired, but Maddox had already gone. Ham looked at his watch and touching Macduff's shoulder, signalled that they must go. They ran for the stairwell. They raced up the stairs and to the chinook which took off as soon as they were aboard.

Ham asked the captain to circle the helicopter so that he could check that John and the FSK team were safely on their boat. Maddox still worried Ham, but he hoped that wherever he was hiding, he would perish with the base.

John, who had been first down the rope, was preparing to start the craft. Matthias Berland was down and storing their gear. Karoline was abseiling down to the boat, and Munsen was checking that the top was secure. Suddenly a powerboat shot out of a concealed entrance. Maddox was the passenger; one of his henchmen was at the controls. Maddox's face curled up in hate as he mouthed obscenities. He turned and fired at the figure on the rope with a machine pistol. Karoline shuddered as bullets stitched across her back. She fell back and hung from the abseiling descender like a rag doll. Maddox changed his aim to the ORC and sprayed it as he rode past, catching John who clasped his shoulder and fell backwards. Berland quickly recovered from his initial shock and returned fire at Maddox's craft as it raced on. Ham was horrified.

Ham ordered the chinook down after the powerboat. The chinooks pilot had seen the attack and gladly obeyed. The helicopter banked down and chased the fleeing boat. The powerboat was fast, and it was getting faster, fifty, sixty, seventy-five kilometres per hour. The chinook chased the boat. The chinook was much faster. As the chinook overtook the powerboat, the minigun whined like a high-speed buzzsaw, and the M60 chattered as they drenched the speeding boat in a deadly carpet of lead. A red mist exploded from the bloody mass that had been the driver and the boat shattered into driftwood, flotsam on the sea. Maddox was gone. One minute he was the next he was gone. They looked, but he did not reappear.

Meanwhile, Munsen came down the rope and checked Hauger. She was dead as Ham and Munsen's second sight had predicted. He lowered her to the boat where Berland was giving first aid to a protesting Paterson.

The chinook returned to the island. Munsen informed Ham that Karoline was dead and that John would live to fight another day.

The chinook picked up the ORC, and they set off for Tiree. Ham and Magnus looked back at the island.

As they began to fly away from the island, it suddenly expanded. From looking like a giant nipple, it became a dome. Smoke and flames shot out of cracks. Even above the roar of the helicopter, they heard the whump and groan of the explosion. When it had grown as much as it could, it imploded collapsing in on itself with a thunderous crash. Despite the wind of the helicopter flight, they felt the shockwave rocking the chinook and dangling ORC.

The island looked like a volcano with high walls surrounding a sunken middle. This one was going to confuse the geologists.

They parked the ORC with Mathias guarding Løtnant Karoline Hauger's body wrapped in a sheet, near the island and went to refuel for the sad journey back to HMNB Clyde.

EPILOGUE

Janice Miller found life boring without a boyfriend. Her girlfriends were great fun, but she needed a boyfriend to satisfy the need to be held and touched by someone who cared for her and wanted her.

She had taken the day trip down to Millport from Glasgow on impulse. She had lunch at the Ritz Café and finding out that Millport was not much fun alone had hired a bike and set off around the island. She was more than halfway around, and although the sights were beautiful, she found it unfulfilling alone.

Near Skate Bay she saw a bike lying by the side of the road. Curious, she lay hers beside it and wandered off down the pathway towards the shore.

"Looking for someone," a voice came. It made Janice jump. She turned and saw a young man lying on a flat rock. Dark haired and green-eyed, he lay propped up on his elbow, casually observing her. He smiled.

"What are you doing here?" she asked.

"Silly question? I'm enjoying the view. You?"

"What are you looking at?"

"The navy is doing something out there. Divers are in and out of the water. Cranes are lifting stuff, all covered in tarpaulins. Must be all very hush-hush." She looked out offshore at the goings-on. "I'm Andrew," he introduced himself.

"I'm Janice," Suddenly, Janice's day trip was getting better. Andrew made space for her on the red tartan rug.

Ham, Macduff and John said their sad farewells on the quiet side of an RAF airbase to Major Munsen and Serjantmajor Berland as they departed on a Royal Norwegian Air Force C-130J-30 with the coffined remains of Løtnant Karoline Hauge.

Rob and Jaimie were returned to HMNB a few days later by a US Navy SH-60 Seahawk helicopter. They returned to the Royal Marine Base Poole. Ham travelled down and spoke with them a few days later, offering them both full-time positions in the department on his team. Jaimie said that he wanted to stay with the SBS, but he would gladly return if he were ever needed again. Ham said he was to consider himself on call. Ham was not surprised; Rob had already told him that Jaimie was keen on a girl in Poole and that he was planning to get engaged soon.

Turning to Rob, he raised his left eyebrow in question. Rob paused as he thought about it for a moment, then he said he only had another year left in the SBS, and if the offer were still standing, he would take a rain-check until then. Ham agreed. He wanted as few people as possible wandering around with knowledge of the cryptids as possible, so he would gladly use them in the future as the need arose. Ham said that he would welcome Rob back into the fold when he was ready, while secretly knowing that he would try to get him to move earlier than Rob suggested.

Ham had tackled John during their trip to the RAF base to say goodbye to the Norwegians. John, with his arm in a sling, was still technically attached to naval intelligence, Ham had asked him if he wanted to stay there, go back to the SBS, or become a member of the team. John said that, apart from getting shot, he had enjoyed his time, that he thought the work would be interesting and that he would like to transfer to the department. Pursing his lips and nodding, Ham said the general would arrange it.

Ham gave Macduff a week's leave, with the understanding that he wanted a final decision when she returned if she wanted to stay in the department. He knew that she had been upset about being used as bait to draw out Maddox's goons and further angered when she realised that she had been under suspicion. The fact that the true traitor had met with a 'lethal accident' did not help. She took the week's leave, stating on her return that she had already decided to stay, but needed a break to get her head together. It was a different world that he was asking her to enter, that was part of the attraction, but it still frightened her a bit. Anyway, she said, having lumped the big boss's son, her future in the regular Army was going to be somewhat limited, and if Ham was serious about mentoring her in MIC, she was interested in being mentored.

Janet offered to move in with Ham which he politely refused with some barely hidden alarm. As a semi-retired colonel in Military Intelligence, he was more comfortable as a semi-retired widower. He arranged for Janet to move into a safe house with Macduff. Janet still came round to Ham's most days and took over Ham's domestic personal arrangements. Compromises made, everyone was happy. Major and Princess seemed happy with the arrangement, Major lapping up the affectionate rubs, and Princess moaning that Ham never fed her; a lie which they were all aware. Ham seemed puzzled by the whole turn of events. He did not understand why Janet had wanted to live with him. Who the heck wants to move in with a grumpy old guy? He did find her incredibly attractive, especially for a two-hundred-year-old, but the whole idea was preposterous, she was his late friend's widow. Besides, his late wives were still wandering around the apartment; not all the time, just when they felt like it, it seemed. Was he crazy, or was he seeing and hearing them?

He started to wear his pouch again so that he could feel that no-one was looking over his shoulder. He would take it off when he had to.

As Ham wrote out a detailed report with recommendations, he wondered who would read the report; the PM? The general already knew what had happened as he had arranged the logistics for most of it. The group of people who knew what the MIC did was very small. As Ham printed the report which would be picked up and hand-delivered by a courier, he wondered where all the reports he filed in the past were stored. They would make for interesting reading by any historian; very interesting.

Finishing his mug of tea, Ham sat back and relaxed. He was in semi-retirement, and he intended to enjoy it. He guessed the general would turn up in the not too distant future to give him his next mission, but that did not mean that Ham would make it easy for the old goat Ham knew it would not be a long wait. He read in that morning's paper that they were delaying the building of some fish farms between the Hebridian islands and the mainland of Scotland due to the rumour of problems with 'sea-fairies'. Ham wondered if it was the 'Blue Men of the Minch'. He knew that some rumours were not rumours.

Getting up, he stood in the bay window, Major asleep on the rug and the kitten asleep on the dog. The sun shone, the ferry plied back and forth across the Clyde, and relative normality returned; for now.

Printed in Poland
by Amazon Fulfillment
Poland Sp. z o.o., Wrocław